SEDUCED BY DENIAL

BROTHERHOOD PROTECTORS WORLD

STACEY WILK

Twisted Page Press LLC

BROTHERHOOD PROTECTORS

ORIGINAL SERIES BY ELLE JAMES

Brotherhood Protectors Series

Montana SEAL (#1)

Bride Protector SEAL (#2)

Montana D-Force (#3)

Cowboy D-Force (#4)

Montana Ranger (#5)

Montana Dog Soldier (#6)

Montana SEAL Daddy (#7)

Montana Ranger's Wedding Vow (#8)

Montana SEAL Undercover Daddy (#9)

Cape Cod SEAL Rescue (#10)

Montana SEAL Friendly Fire (#11)

Montana SEAL's Mail-Order Bride (#12)

SEAL Justice (#13)

Ranger Creed (#14)

Delta Force Rescue (#15)

Montana Rescue (Sleeper SEAL)

Hot SEAL Salty Dog (SEALs in Paradise)

Hot SEAL Hawaiian Nights (SEALs in Paradise)

Seduced by Denial
(Close Protection Series #1)

Brotherhood Protectors World

Stacey Wilk

To my readers.
Without you, all my stories would fall on deaf ears.

CHAPTER 1

Bebe Murano hated her husband. She had no idea how she had ended up where she was. Well, she had some idea. She wasn't clueless.

Thousands of people standing behind barricades yelled loud enough to break the sound barrier. The hot June sun did nothing to deter their stomping feet that shook the earth. They wanted to meet Bebe and Stuart. She and Stuart had signed autographs and taken photos for two hours. Her mouth hurt from the fake smiling. The fans needed to believe she and Stuart liked each other.

One minute she was just some woman no one had heard of who enjoyed fixing up houses, and the next minute she was one half of a husband and wife design team loved by millions. The audience enjoyed their banter and their designs more. It was a dream come true. A dream she had worked her ass off for and had deserved. The kick in the pants was the success came after the divorce papers had been finalized. Success now equaled Stuart, and she was tired of it.

"That's it, folks. Thanks for coming. Don't forget our new season starts in September." Stuart flashed his implant-filled smile.

The crowd roared. She wanted to get out of there. Cheers and applause crested. She didn't like crowds anymore, not since the stalker. The vibration made it hard to hear even when Stuart leaned in and said something in her ear. All she got was the cloying scent of his cologne. He put his hand on the small of her back as if he still had the right. She didn't shrug him off for fear a fan would notice. She bit the inside of her cheek to fend off the repulsion of his touch.

The heat had made her sweat through her shirt. Her stomach begged for food. She hadn't eaten for hours. And she had filled her time with Stuart quota for the day. Other than filming and publicity events, they never went near each other.

After today, she wouldn't have to see him for a few weeks. She couldn't wait. They turned from the crowd and to the direction of the cars waiting for them.

A large crack whipped through the air, splitting it in half. Screams erupted. The force of a freight train slammed into her, knocking her off balance. A sharp pain shot through her shoulder. Something warm and wet ran down her arm and between her fingers. Her mind couldn't catch up to what her eyes registered.

People ran. Someone threw a heavy arm over her shoulders and pushed her head down as he dragged her away.

"Stay down, Bebe. I've got you." She recognized the deep voice but couldn't place the name of the security guard hired by the network.

He whisked her away from the screams and the crowd. They ran to the town car waiting for them. He shoved her inside and dove in after her. The thing she feared the most was happening.

"Get the hell out of here. Now, damn it," he said to the driver. "She needs a hospital."

BEBE'S LEGS dangled off the side of the hospital bed. Her arm was secured with a sling, and her shoulder ached deep in the bone. The bullet had grazed the shoulder muscle and had done minimal damage, but the pain made her head spin. The air conditioning pumped on over drive in the emergency room. She wondered if the unit was old and outdated or if the docs and nurses liked artic temperatures.

It had been hours since she had been escorted here. She wanted to go home to a hot bath and a shot of whiskey, but she needed some answers. The first one being who did this. She didn't like the possibilities. Since her recent rise to fame, more people knew who she was, and not everyone liked her. One person liked her too much.

"How much longer, Dad?" Her voice scraped against her dry throat. She reached for the plastic pink cup on the table beside the bed. The cool water didn't do much to soothe the discomfort.

Her father stood in the corner of the curtained area with his hands in his pockets. The vertical crease between his brows deepened, and he rocked slightly on the balls of his feet. "Please let the detective tell us what he knows, Bebe. Then I can take you home." His voice held the calm resolve she had come to expect and rely on. His broad shoulders had always carried her burdens. The only sign he might be stressed was the thin line of his lips hiding under his thick mustache.

Detective Adams flipped his notebook closed and held her gaze. His gold shield hung around his neck on a long chain and caught the fluorescent light each time he moved.

"I'm sorry to have to tell you this, Ms. Murano, but the man we arrested today is your stalker." What was left of his hair formed a widow's peak at the top of his hairline. He had frown lines etched between his brows, but his brown eyes shone with tenderness.

"Why are you sorry about that?" Relief washed

over her like a hot spray coming from a brand-new rain showerhead. They had finally caught the man who had been torturing her for months.

At first her stalker seemed innocent enough. He'd sent a few emails saying he liked the show and that he thought she was pretty. She had made the mistake of responding, but the show's success was new and she had wanted her fans to think she was approachable. The number of emails increased until he was sending hundreds a week. Each one growing in anger and threats until he said he wanted to kidnap her.

"The only thing I'm sorry about is he showed up at your event," Detective Adams said. "He could've hurt a lot of people. We got lucky on that point. He confessed immediately. The good news is he'll be off the street now and won't be able to hurt anyone any longer."

"And the bad news is?" her father said.

"It appears the gunshot was intended for Ms. Murano's husband. Benjamin Morris stated after his rights had been read that he meant to kill Mr. Young to prove to you how much he loved you."

"Oh boy." Her father pressed his lips together and dragged his gaze away.

"I don't understand. Why try to shoot Stuart?" No matter how much she and Stuart didn't get along, she didn't want anything bad to happen to him. Until today, the stalker hadn't ever mentioned Stuart.

"It's not uncommon for a stalker to try and hurt

someone else as proof of their affection. I'm sure you remember the incident where Ronald Reagan was shot."

"But I'm not that famous."

"It doesn't matter. Mr. Morris was an obsessed fan. Stalker crimes have been on the up rise since the advent of social media. Access to too many people. People who don't have to be the president." Detective Adams shoved his small notebook into the back pocket of his jeans.

"Now, what does she do?" her father said.

"Get on with your life." Detective Adams held his palms up as if the answer were so simple.

"How am I supposed to do that?" Sure they had caught the guy, but would someone else be lurking in the shadows next? Had she made a mistake by becoming a public figure after all?

"That's entirely up to you, but I assure you, you won't hear from Benjamin Morris again. If you'll excuse me." Detective Adams ducked past her father and out the curtain.

"Dad?"

"Yeah, sweetie?" Her father continued to rock on his heels. She and her father had been facing the world together ever since her mother died in a shootout right on the gang-infested street they used to live on. Part of the reason she had agreed to do the television show even after she and Stuart divorced was to ensure her father never had to worry about money again.

"How am I supposed to get on with my life? A man tried to kill Stuart and almost killed me instead."

"They caught him."

"I don't want this life anymore. Not if this is what it means." The words floated out as easily as setting a table for reveal day. If it had been that easy, maybe she had never wanted this kind of life after all.

"You're just upset. Don't make any hasty decisions."

"Damn straight, I'm upset." She hopped off the table and waited a second for the room to straighten out. "I'm through with television and Stuart. I hate that arrogant bastard any way. He's impossible. I did like the success until I ended up with a bullet through my shoulder. But I like my life better."

"Bebe, let me take you back to my place for a day or two. Take some time to think about what you're saying. You have money now. You live a nice life. A life I couldn't give you. Don't throw it all away over some lunatic."

"Dad, the life I had growing up with you and Mom was the best. Fame and fortune can't top that." She adjusted the sling and tried not to wince from the pain.

Her father stared off in the distance and shrugged with a heavy sigh. "Maybe. I don't know. But now you don't have to worry about bullets flying every time you step outside your door."

"I did today."

"It's not the same thing."

"I'll stay with you for a few days, but I won't change my mind. I quit."

CHAPTER 2

READE BREWER GLANCED at the typewritten letter on standard white paper and covered in a plastic protective sheet. A stalker wrote a threatening letter to some famous actress. Reade didn't pay attention to pop culture so the actress's name meant little to him. His interests lay in places other than film and television.

"You ready to go?" Lincoln slid out of the booth.

He followed with a nod. Lincoln had picked the dinner spot. People in varying shapes and ages filled the bar from every corner. Music pumped out of an old jukebox like blood from a torn artery, forcing everyone to raise their voices to be heard. A great place to have a discussion in public when the conversation needed to stay private. Hide in plain sight kind of thing. No one paid any attention to two nondescript guys having dinner and minding their own business.

But the rest of the conversation would take place out of sight. He walked with Linc in silence until they stood at the farthest spot in the parking lot. The summer night air was cool and dry against his skin. He shoved his hands into the pockets of his jeans and leaned against the grill of his pickup.

"Stalker cases are constantly increasing, Brewer. The calls won't stop coming in from agents wanting protection for their clients or the celebs themselves. Everyone wants to keep their needs quiet. I'm glad you're willing to come work for me." Lincoln raked his hand through his long hair. Linc had been out of the Rangers five minutes and had grown his hair to his shoulders. Linc had some great hair for a guy his age. Not that Reade would ever say it. Linc's hair was Linc's business.

"You asked and I came." That's how it would always be between him and Linc.

"Hank Patterson assigned me the task of gathering a new team for the Brotherhood Protectors to guard more celebrities like the one I'm assigning you to watch."

"I don't understand why anyone wants to give up so much of their privacy." He understood the money was pretty good in that line of work, but no amount of money could make him live a life where more people than not wanted a piece of him.

"I don't either, but it keeps us in business." Linc flashed a grin.

A couple holding hands interrupted the conversation with their approaching presence. The two lovebirds looked at each other, oblivious to anything else, and shared muffled words that made the lady laugh. They didn't notice him and Linc until they were a car away. Reade wanted to tell them to be aware of their surroundings, but he only nodded at the guy who nearly dropped his keys when he laid a wide-eyed stare on him and Linc. Can't be too careful.

After the car pulled away, he said, "Thanks for the opportunity to join your team. These past three years adjusting have been hell."

"Getting back into civilian life isn't always easy. You'll get the hang of it. The work will keep you busy and out of your own thoughts. You can continue to use the skills you honed all those years instead of hopping around from one construction site to another." Linc flipped his keys around his finger.

"Seemed like good work at the time." He enjoyed being outside and building things. After he got home from his twenty in the Army, he didn't have any idea what to do with himself. Construction was as good as any job. He was able to travel to find work. Or not settle down was more like it.

Any town he went to closed around him like a vise before long. As soon as he noticed the grip on his chest, he packed up and found another job. He suspected Winter, Montana would be the same soon enough.

Becoming a bodyguard for this special organization seemed more like being paid to babysit and wear his gun than a difficult job. It sure wasn't like being an Army Ranger. But Lincoln wanted him on board, and he would never tell a brother no.

"I've got four of our other men from our company on the payroll too."

He and Linc had been friends for what seemed like forever. Now, he reported to Linc again.

"We're all working on this close protection group?" He didn't bother to ask who the other men were. Whoever Linc picked would be a man who held the Ranger creed close.

"You'll each have your own assignment, but if you need backup, I'll come running with whoever I grab. You're in good hands."

He trusted Linc with his life. He wasn't worried about backup. If he even needed it, which he doubted, Linc would provide the best.

"Do I have to pick her up?" He and Linc had reviewed the case notes at the start of dinner. His assignment was some fixer-upper television show woman. Like the actress mentioned in the email Linc just showed him, Reade had no idea who Bebe Murano was.

"She's already here. She bought a small house on

the lake. I'll text you the address." Linc pulled out his phone and tapped the screen.

"If the guy after her was arrested, why is she hiring a guard?" The file had said the man confessed. Miss Celebrity should be ready to get back in the limelight and not want to hang out on a lake in rural Montana.

"She's spooked. Someone like her isn't used to getting shot at."

"I suspect not." Someone like this television star was probably used to people doing whatever she demanded. He would make sure to stay out of her way.

"There's no end date to the gig. You have to stay on her until she pulls the plug. Can I count on that?"

"What are you saying, Linc?" He didn't like the possibility his friend and former commander thought he'd let him down.

He slid his gaze back toward the center of the parking lot. A group of women in short skirts and high heels leaned on each other as they pranced toward their cars. He hoped none of those women had been drinking too much.

"I'm saying you have a reputation for pulling up roots after a while. That can't happen anymore."

"I've never let you down before." Two men, one in a leather jacket, laughed and stumbled as they went in the same direction as those women and tightened their distance. Summer nights might be cooler than the days in Montana, but not cool enough for leather.

"We aren't at war now."

"Hey." He called out toward the women then turned back to Linc. "I'll be right back." He marched over to the ladies. "Ma'am. Did you drop your phone?" He held his own phone out because it was the only prop he had.

The women turned in his direction and stopped, almost colliding with the men. Each lady fumbled inside a purse, finding her phone. But the men went another way. Maybe he was being overly cautious, but he didn't like to ignore the details or the cold shiver down his spine. He jogged back to Linc.

"Sorry about that. I didn't like what I thought I saw. Anyway, you have my word. I won't let you down."

"Good enough. And good call on that." Linc pointed into the belly of the parking lot. "You're on duty twenty-four seven. She's got a small cottage on the property for you to sleep in. The work shouldn't be any big deal, but if you need a day off, shoot a text. I'll send one of the other men on our new team over to relieve you. I also have Jax Montero, Quint Porter, or Zane Cutler available."

He had met Montero and Porter before, but he didn't know this Cutler guy. "Cutler okay?"

"He's young, but he's good."

"Okay, then." He was ready to get to work. His

skin itched for the old days in the Army when he had his orders to follow and knew exactly what was expected of him.

"You'll check in each day." Linc emphasized the order with a nod. Same Linc as always.

"I know the drill, Linc." And was glad for it again.

"I'm happy you're doing this. Not just for me, but for you too."

"I'm fine."

"So you've said."

"Linc, stop busting my balls. I'm fine. I'll do the work and stick around until you tell me to get packing." He was fine. He missed his brotherhood in the Army. He missed being tied to something like a town or a home, but he doubted he'd find what he needed in Winter. This town was just a stop to another destination.

"Okay, then." Linc stuck out his hand.

Reade took it and gave Linc a hard shake. "I'll check in as soon as I meet this woman."

"Bebe Murano. Bebe is short for Benedetta."

"Right. Sure." A fancy name for a fancy lady. He would've preferred to be holed up in the woods in a tent. He suspected this Bebe Murano wouldn't fair well roughing it.

The last woman in his life thought camping meant a fully stocked sprawling cabin. She wouldn't lift a finger, never mind something like a hammer. He was through with women anyway. Too many expectations. He wasn't suited for long term relationships, and he hadn't met too many women willing to keep things uncomplicated for long. They wanted things from him he wasn't willing to give.

"Listen, I know this assignment seems like a walk in the park compared to what we've seen on the front lines, but you could still be dealing with an unstable individual when it comes to this stalker."

"But you said he's in jail."

"Just be prepared for all possibilities."

"Still worrying like an old hen. You want to tuck me in at night too?"

Linc punched his shoulder. "Now who's busting balls? My men's safety is always my first concern."

"Don't worry. I can do this job with my eyes closed."

CHAPTER 3

THE CABIN WASN'T MUCH, but it was hers, and it was tucked away where no one could find her. The place needed a little work. Bebe's hands craved to restain the wood floors, update the kitchen, and bring additional light in by making the windows floor-to-ceiling. The views of the mountains were breathtaking, but she'd be a sitting duck if someone walked up at night. They could see in, but she wouldn't be able to see them. Automatic room darkening shades would have to be installed if she expanded the windows. She'd add sensor lights around the perimeter of the house. And security cameras.

The bodyguard was due to arrive soon. Hiring protection was the peace of mind she needed. It didn't matter that Benjamin Morris was in jail. The months of his threats had taken its toll on her. Every nerve had been scraped raw wondering when he would strike. All the while she and Stuart had fought. She should've left him when she had the chance. Then there would have been no television show and no stalker trying to kill her. She had traded privacy and peace of mind for fame and success If she knew now…

She checked the locks on the front door and the slider out to the back patio. The sun dipped below the tops of the mountains. It would be dark soon. She wished the bodyguard would get there. Once the stars came out, she hunkered down each night. She hadn't gone out to the store or to visit friends after dark since she had been shot. She didn't want to have to show her new employee to his cabin in the dark either. Lighting the path from her place to the extra building would also go on the list of things to do.

Her phone rang. She dug it out of her bag. "Hey, Dad."

"Hi, sweetie. How's it going?"

"Same as yesterday. You don't have to check in every day. I'm doing okay out here." She really was. The space of the property meant people couldn't just walk up to her house if they felt like it. No one was going to come back here unless they knew what they were looking for. The shades on the windows and the sensor lights were just precautions to keep the fears at bay for now.

"I can come out if you want company." Her dad's voice bounced with hopefulness.

"I can't ask you to leave your entire life behind right now. If I need anything, I'll call."

"Did the bodyguard get there?"

"Not yet." She checked the clock over the kitchen window. She hoped he wasn't one who ran late. That wouldn't work for her.

"Oh boy."

"Dad, it's fine." She didn't want him to worry, but no amount of trying to convince hm would work.

She grabbed a glass out of the cabinet and filled it with ice. She got lucky when the cabin came furnished too. It had been a glamping rental, but the owner didn't want to deal with the winters anymore. He had been desperate to sell, and she had come along at the right time. She had sold her place in California, packed up only the things that meant the most to her, and moved to Montana.

"Benedetta, there's something you should know."

The use of her full name sent shivers over her skin. He had used the same sentence when he told her Mom had been shot. "What?"

He took a deep breath. "I don't know how to tell you this."

"Just say it." Her voice shook with fright. She tried to take long deep breaths to calm her hammering heart. He could say anything. Like he decided to move out to Montana too. It didn't have to be bad news.

"Benjamin Morris has been released on a technicality. Detective Adams just called me."

The glass slipped from her hand and shattered on the floor. Ice cubes broke and skidded in opposite directions.

"Bebe, did you hear me?"

"Why did he call you and not me?"

"He tried, but your phone went to voicemail."

She had turned her phone off on the plane and had forgotten until a little while ago. "How did this happen?" The kitchen went out of focus. She blinked several times to shake off the dark corners of her vision.

"The arresting officer filled out the complaint form incorrectly. It wasn't discovered until Morris appeared in court. With the form filled out incorrectly, he walked. I'm sorry."

"Well, have the arresting officer fix the form." How much simpler could it be?

"He retired from the job the week after the incident. He can't change the form now. I wish I had better news. I really am so very sorry."

A groan rumbled in her throat. Her knees let loose, and she folded to the floor among the melting ice. "But what about the attempted murder and the confession?"

"Even though he was caught, he decided to plead not guilty. The morning of his arraignment, his defense attorney brought up the gross error. It's unbelievable, but it's true. He walked. But he doesn't know where you are. Remember that."

She had purposely put the house in a company's name that claimed her mother was the president. Her mother had been dead for two decades. Had that been enough to hide from Morris? Only her father knew where she was, but had she missed something that could lead Benjamin Morris to her?

"What if he finds me?" She pulled her legs into her chest and rested her head on her knees.

"He can't. You'll have round-the-clock protection. That bodyguard won't leave your side. And, Bebe, did you give anymore thought to what we talked about?"

"No guns, Dad. I won't carry a gun around. Forget it. I wish you'd stop bringing it up." Her father had tried to persuade her, but she wouldn't hear of it. She had no idea what to do with a gun. She also didn't want to be responsible for hurting anyone. The bodyguard would have to be enough. She was going to have to trust him. And that thought made her insides shake. Trusting a stranger after having a stalker seemed a bit like an oxymoron.

"Okay, okay. No more gun talk. Are you going to be okay until your bodyguard gets there? What's his name again?"

"Reade Brewer. I'll be okay." She pushed off the floor and stepped around the broken glass. "I have to go, Dad. I'll talk to you tomorrow." She ended the call. Her father was incapable of helping her from where he was.

She just needed to get through the next hour until the bodyguard arrived.

READE COULDN'T REMEMBER the last time he blew a tire. He slapped the steering wheel and cursed. He had already been running late because of traffic and locking down his apartment for the duration of this assignment. After struggling to remove the spare from under the truck bed, he had tacked on almost an hour over his arrival time. Linc had called the client to explain. That didn't make Reade feel any better. An Army Ranger was never late.

The sun had set a mile ago before his tire blew rubber all over the road. Now, he flew past the entrance to the client's property and had to circle back. He would've seen the driveway obscured by some trees in the daylight, but in the dark, it wasn't visible at all. Her instructions to find the blue mailbox did nothing for him at the moment.

He turned onto the drive and activated the high beams. The dirt and gravel path bounced his truck from side to side making the pain in his back ramp up a notch. He had wrenched it while carrying a Ranger brother. That was right before he finished up his twenty. He hated to admit he didn't heal up the way he did when he was in his twenties.

He gripped the wheel tighter to keep the vehicle straight. The land was wooded on either side of him. Not an ounce of the moonlight penetrated those woods. The view of the house was protected by the tall trees with wide branches, but it also gave someone plenty of places to hide. He'd have to check out the area on foot tomorrow. Tonight he wanted to say hello to the client and get some sleep. Babysitting could start at dawn after he had had a strong cup of coffee and some rest for his back.

The space opened up to reveal plenty of flatland and a small cabin with the lights on inside. Ms. Murano must be a night owl. In the distance he could make out another building, most likely his new residence. He'd take a tent and sleep on the ground right now. He pulled up in front of the first cabin and eased out of the truck. Yeah, he was getting old.

The tall grass rustled in the evening breeze. The stars filled the sky with pinholes of light. He inhaled the lake-scented air and craved the separation and space a piece of property like this afforded. After this assignment, he'd look into moving out of that tiny apartment. If he decided Winter or even Montana was the place for him.

He trudged up the front porch. The single porch light caused a puddle of yellow on his boots. He took a deep breath and knocked.

The door swung open while his hand was still in midair.

"Where the hell have you been?" A beautiful woman with a head of black curls spraying in multiple directions and with wild in her eyes stared at him.

He planted his feet, but he had to tilt his head down to meet that fiery gaze. "You must be Bebe Murano. I'm Reade Brewer with the Brotherhood Protectors. I apologize for being late." He pulled his business card out of his shirt pocket. The Brotherhood didn't have shields or badges, though he thought they should. He didn't see the need to mention Linc had called to warn her Reade was running behind.

"You're over two hours late. I've been pacing back and forth wondering when you would arrive. What if something happened?" She glanced at the card then crumpled it in her fist.

"What were you expecting to happen?" It figured she would be raging about his tardiness. She probably expected her employees to be at her beck and call. He could put up with that from one of his commanders, even Linc, but not this spoiled lady.

She marched away. "Come in and close the door. I don't like standing in the open."

He did as she requested but didn't lock it. She dropped down on the couch and ran her hands over her face. Her audible exhales seemed to indicate she wanted to regulate her breath but couldn't. Linc had said she seemed to be handling the stalker incident in stride, but maybe that had been an act. Maybe she was afraid. And afraid of him too.

"Ms. Murano, I am sorry about not arriving on time. That won't happen again. I can do a check of the property if that will make you feel better."

"What would make me feel better is a strong whiskey, but I don't have any." She jumped up and went to the window, then dashed away to the far corner of the room.

"I can drive you into town tomorrow. In the meantime, I can make sure all the windows are locked."

"Does a locked window actually stop someone?" She ran her hand through her hair, sending it in more directions as if that were even possible.

"Maybe you'd feel better in a more populated area. Is there somewhere you'd like to go?" He didn't need his honed instincts to tell him something more than her displeasure with him being late was going on. Maybe she'd had a fight with her boyfriend or she just found out her daily massage had to be canceled.

He wasn't being fair to the pretty Ms. Murano. She would have every reason to be upset after what she'd been through, but he was rarely wrong when he read people. Something new developed recently.

"I don't want to be around people. And I don't

know if I can be alone." She slouched and shoved her hands under her arms.

He could relate to what she had said. Since he'd been home, he didn't want to be alone or with anyone either. His restlessness was part of the reason he continued to move. "It's your call."

"I don't have anywhere else to go. And he'll find me no matter where I am." She stared at the darkened window instead of looking at him.

"Excuse me?" He took a small step closer. He didn't want to frighten her off.

"Benjamin Morris was released from jail." She wasn't blinking.

"When?" He needed to call Linc. The Brotherhood had missed that important new piece of information. This job could end up being more complicated than planned. Unless there was no way Benjamin Morris could find her.

"I'm not sure. Yesterday. Today maybe. My father called a few hours ago to tell me. Can he find me here?"

"I hope not, but I'll check to see what kind of a trail you left. In the meantime, why don't you pull those shades down and try to relax. I'll walk the property and keep watch, then I'll call my boss."

"No."

"You don't want me to walk the property? Or call my boss? Both are part of my job."

"Please don't leave me alone." Her pupils were

dilated, and the color had drained from her face, making her lips as pale as her skin.

"Ms. Murano—"

"Bebe. Or Benedetta if you want to be formal, but not Ms. Murano. That makes me sound stuck-up."

A warmth slid over him, and he wasn't sure where it came from. Maybe it was the wide-eyed stare that said she needed help. "Bebe, my hunch is you're a smart lady. I doubt Benjamin Morris has come looking for you, but if it makes you feel better, call my cell and stay on the line while I wander around a little." So much for saying hello and grabbing a few winks. This was no babysitting job.

"I don't have your number."

"It's on that card you squashed into a little ball." He nodded in the direction of the white blob on the coffee table.

"I'm sorry." The corner of her mouth turned up, and some of the light came back into her eyes. She was petite, but her shoulders and biceps were sculpted. Probably from all the physical labor she did. At least that part of her show was genuine.

She had on some kind of black yoga pants that stopped mid-calf—also toned—and showed off her thin ankles and pink polished toenails. That warmth that had slid over him a moment ago moved to his low belly. Okay, she was attractive, and he had experienced a bit of a dry spell lately.

She smoothed out the card. "There. I'll call you

while you check things out. I feel a little better. Thank you. I'm sorry I was short with you. That's not like me. I'm…well…I'm usually nicer than that." She looked up at him through her thick lashes, and a blush crept across her cheeks.

"Don't worry about it."

He went out the door and closed it behind him. His phone vibrated in his pocket. Ms. Murano was right on schedule.

Sleepless nights were in his future. For more reasons than one.

CHAPTER 4

BEBE COULDN'T SLEEP. She checked the time on her phone again. The numbers barely changed. Before the stalker, she slept like a log. Construction could be going on in the next room and she wouldn't hear a thing. Now, even with a big bodyguard only feet away, she couldn't make sleep show up.

Having Reade's presence in her house should make her feel more in control of something, but it didn't. She had insisted he sleep on the couch instead of in his own cabin. He hadn't argued, but he had eyed the small couch with a lift of his brow. He was tall and well-built. Not like a man who spent hours in the gym, but more like a guy who had spent his days doing hard labor. The square jaw covered in a salt-and-pepper beard only added to his rough exterior. He wore the rugged man look, with the creases around his light eyes, and the permanent line between his brows, like a freshly renovated log cabin.

She threw her legs over the side of the bed. The wood floor was cool beneath her feet. The moonlight slipped through the sides of the curtains. The king-size bed took up most of the space in here, but the past owner managed to get a dresser and a stand-up mirror into two corners. She could break out the back wall about ten feet and add French doors out to a deck. Bring the outside in. Maybe even add a master bath.

That was if she even stayed here. She wasn't sure if she'd made the right decision by coming. The impulsive buy and move might backfire. Maybe the other side of the country would have been better.

She padded down the short hallway toward the soft light spilling in from the living area. She wouldn't wake Reade if he'd fallen asleep, but if he was awake, a little company might be nice.

She peeked around the corner, expecting to see him with his head back on the couch, his mouth open and his eyes closed. Instead, he'd propped his feet up on the couch, and he was reading an actual book. He had removed the shirt he wore earlier. A black sleeveless shirt exposed an elaborate tattoo on his left shoulder. His wearing rugged well was an understatement.

"Having trouble sleeping?" His voice made her jump. He hadn't budged from his spot on the couch.

"How did you know I was here?" A heat crept up her neck.

"It's my job. Is everything okay?" He dropped his feet and the book and faced her. His shoulders seemed broader from this view. His waist narrowed into his jeans. The scowl on his face would have scared her if he wasn't working for her.

"I couldn't sleep. I guess you can't either?" She had nothing to fear from this man. His company had come highly recommended. The Brotherhood Protectors had an impressive reputation.

"Do you want to come out from behind the wall?" He arched a brow. The hint of a smile tugged at his lips. He looked good in a smile.

"I'm not hiding." She tugged at the bottom of her pajama shirt.

"You're peering around the corner as if you expect someone to rush after you. Everything is locked up tight. No one is outside. I would've heard it."

"How long have you been a bodyguard?"

He scratched his beard. "I'm a new member of the Brotherhood Protectors, if that's what you're asking."

"Where did you work before?" She brushed past him to get to the kitchen and caught a whiff of his masculine scent mixed with pine.

The light from the living area offered her enough glow to move around in the kitchen. The space was small like the rest of the house. Almost too small for someone Reade's size to fit in comfortably. He must

31

be uncomfortable on the couch, but disquiet wouldn't allow her to send him through the yard to his place. At least not for tonight.

"The Army."

"That gave you the skill set to be a bodyguard?" She pulled two mugs from the cabinet and held one up for him. He shook his head.

"I would say so. My boss seems to think so too."

"That means you can shoot a gun." She shook the tea kettle and found it empty. She didn't want the tea as much as she wanted something to do. Whenever she had been stressed, she found wood that needed sanding or wallpaper that needed to be torn down. First thing in the morning, she'd start a project. That had been the plan to heal when she arrived. She couldn't allow Benjamin Morris to take that from her too.

"I can hold my own with a firearm."

"I hate guns." She understood hunting as a sport, but why did an average person think he or she needed to own an armory in their home? What was that going to accomplish other than hurt?

"Then I guess it's a good thing for you that you don't have to carry one. Is my gun going to be a problem for you?"

"Where is your gun?" She scanned the living area but didn't see anything.

He lifted the leg of his jeans, revealing a gun and holster tied to his ankle. "I also have a shoulder holster, but I didn't think I'd need it tonight. That gun is secured in my duffel." He pointed to the large black bag in the corner.

"Why is that?" She filled the kettle and put it over the flame on the stove.

"After you went to bed, I did some checking. Your house and this property can't be traced to you without some real effort. Effort a man like Benjamin Morris could try to extend but won't be smart enough to see to the end. You did a good job of hiding. He isn't coming here tonight or tomorrow or anytime soon."

"How can you be sure? He hasn't given up on me yet."

"He knew how to find you before. You were on television. All over social media. Even the bottom of your newsletter gave a physical address. You made it easy for him. Now you finally figured out if you want to stay safe, you need to stay private."

"Wait a second. Are you trying to say because I have a successful television show and lots of fans that I asked for this man to stalk me and try to shoot me?"

"He tried to shoot your ex-husband. You got nailed by a ricochet. He doesn't want to kill you. He thinks he's in love with you. Your ex has more to worry about than you do. Or any other man you're involved with."

"For once, Stuart didn't do anything wrong. He brings entertainment to people's lives. He's actually kind of funny when he isn't being an ass. And we're good at what we do. The opportunity came along for us to help so many people live in the house of their dreams. Neither Stuart nor I should be punished for that by some nutcase stalker."

"You had to know what you and your ex-husband were giving up by being on television. I know you want to have your fame and fortune and your privacy, but it doesn't work that way."

"I was going after my dream. Haven't you had a dream worth pursuing?" She grabbed a tea bag and plopped it into the mug while water boiled.

"My dreams have been a lot simpler." He smirked and arched that brow again.

"I don't appreciate you sitting in judgment of me."

"We all judge all the time. It just doesn't feel like judgment when you agree." He dropped back on the couch and retrieved his book.

Heat flushed her face. This guy was supposed to protect her not give her a lecture in the downside to being a celebrity. He had no right to make assumptions of her without knowing her whole story which she wasn't about to tell him.

She wanted to grab that book and toss it across the room. But she wouldn't give him the satisfaction of knowing he'd upset her with his dismissive behavior. She thought maybe they could be company for each other while they had to be together. Clearly, she had been wrong.

With a square of her shoulders, she marched past him.

"Don't go away mad."

The whistle of the tea kettle interfered with her clever, witty response. She slammed the bedroom door on his baritone laugh.

CHAPTER 5

BEBE WOKE with a start and for a second couldn't remember where she was. Then it hit her. She threw an arm over her eyes. Life's complications did not come with a set of directions. She had only wanted to feel safe while she decided what to do about her television show. Safety was an illusion much like control.

She could sign over all the show rights to Stuart and let him do what he wanted, but the network preferred the husband and wife duo even if they were divorced. Word would leak soon that they weren't married any longer, but the network was certain they could still draw an audience. The numbers showed she and Stuart were likeable in their own ways. On camera they faked getting along pretty well.

Or she could start filming with him so the first episode of the new season would air in time. That would put her back in the spotlight just like Reade had accused her of. Every time she stepped in front of the camera, she gave some stranger the chance to torment her.

What she wanted more than anything was to continue to fix up houses and watch people's faces as she made their dreams come true. Thanks to the success of the television show, she was doing that on a large scale. She helped people who wouldn't otherwise have been able to help themselves.

Fans from all over the country emailed her pictures of the designs they'd tried in their own homes because she had inspired them. Their show had brought families back together because they believed she and Stuart did everything from the heart and it made them want to try too. Most of *from the heart* was true. At least for her.

The sun had started the day and was already filling the bedroom with enough light to push her out of bed. She didn't know what to say to Reade after last night's argument. Maybe they didn't have to talk at all. It wasn't as if they'd be friends.

She raced through a shower, pulled her hair back in a ponytail, and went in search of some coffee.

The living area and kitchen were empty as if no one had been there all night. Even his black bag was gone. A fire burned in her belly. Had he quit without saying anything? He wasn't supposed to leave her alone without warning.

The front door swung open. She jumped. Reade

strode into the house with a drink tray holding two to-go cups and a white paper bag tucked under his arm. He had traded his clothes from last night for a faded red t-shirt that covered his tattoo and black jeans hugging his solid legs. A silver chunky wallet chain hung from his belt and to his back pocket. She sucked in a breath and tried not to stare at the handsome man with menace rolling off him.

He narrowed his eyes when he saw her. "You're up." He put the drink tray and the bag on the table.

"Where were you?" Of course, she was awake. He saw her, didn't he?

He pointed at the table as if it should be obvious.

"You're not supposed to leave my side."

"I didn't. Well, except to go to my cabin and take a shower. I did a clean sweep of the perimeter first. I also enabled a smart security camera system this morning. I can watch all sides of your house from my phone."

"I didn't hear any drilling,"

"No drilling needed. The cameras can be placed anywhere. I used your planters outside the front and back doors. The software has facial recognition so it can alert me if someone unfamiliar approaches the house."

"So, we'll know if someone comes to the door before they get there?"

"Not exactly, but it will alert me if the face isn't you or me. What I'd like to do is install something at the start of the drive to alert us when a car turns in. That will cost you, so it's up to you."

"Can I think about that?" The idea had merit. All his extra measures gave her a small sense of ease. She could afford the extra security, but she didn't know if she wanted to stay in the house indefinitely. She wanted to be sure Benjamin Morris couldn't find her before she made that decision. "How did you get that?" She pointed to the offerings on the table.

"Delivery."

"Who delivers out here?"

"Let's say it's a perk of my job." He held up a cup to her. "I didn't know how you took your coffee. You had milk and sugar here."

"Thank you for the coffee. That was very kind of you." The heat of the coffee seeped through the cup and warmed her. Or maybe it was Reade's gesture and the sexy stare in his light eyes as he watched her. She needed to stop thinking words like sexy and Reade in the same sentence. She didn't know this man.

"Hey, about last night—"

"You were right. I apologize." He held up a hand.

"I don't mind if you have an opinion about my line of work. I need to get a thicker skin, that's all."

"I'm here to do a job. Your personal life is none of my concern. What do you have planned for today?"

The abrupt subject change made her head spin. If that's how he wanted it, then she could be all business too. But bringing her breakfast seemed more than just a professional courtesy. Or she had been so lonely lately she had misinterpreted his actions.

"I haven't decided. I would like to take a walk around the lake. Would that be okay?" She was ready to start a project, but the view from the lake and some quiet time would help inspire her with what project to start with.

"Whatever you want. I'll keep you six feet in front of me the entire time. When do you want to leave?" He checked his big black watch.

"After breakfast?" She reached for the bag.

"As you wish. I'll be on the porch when you're ready."

"You aren't going to eat with me?" She tried to keep the disappointment out of her voice but hadn't succeed. She brought his cold shoulder on. Now she'd have to deal with it.

"No, ma'am. My duties aren't to fraternize. I'll be outside." He closed the door behind him without a look back.

She sank into the chair at the kitchen table. She had been surrounded by so many people for work, but none of them really cared about her. They were all nice enough; except when it came down to it, they only wanted what she could do for them, and that included her ex-husband. It had been ages since someone liked her for her. Reade Brewer wasn't going to be that person either. But the idea had been nice for a nanosecond before she came down the hall last night and got mad at him.

She took the coffee and the bag and went outside. Reade leaned against her car. He stopped with the cup halfway to his lips. He pushed off the side and met her by the porch.

"I won't let you get too far ahead of me, but if you decide to break out in a run, give me a heads-up. I don't have on my running shoes."

"Why would I try to get away from you? Wouldn't that be counterproductive from the reason I hired you?" She realized he was being a smart-ass a second too late. Two could play at that game.

"Are you still seething from last night?" He eyed her over the rim of his cup.

"Do you make it a habit of offering your opinion when one wasn't asked for?"

"Afraid so."

"Then I guess I'm still seething." She raised the cup in salute and followed the path down to the lake.

The puffy white clouds and the mountain tops reflected in the deep green water of the lake. She could see straight through to the bottom from her vantage point on the edge of the boat dock. She might have to consider getting a boat if she stayed. The sun warmed her skin and eased some of the stress from her shoulders. The outdoors always had a way of making her feel better when nothing else would. It was why she always enlarged windows in their renos and let in as much light and nature as possible.

She wanted to take some pictures of the lake and the white-tipped mountains in the background with her phone, a little hobby she took up recently to also relieve stress, but she was juggling the bag and the coffee. The photos would have to wait for another time.

"What do I owe you for the breakfast?" she said over her shoulder.

"It's on me."

"I can't let you buy me food. You work for me." She never wanted someone on her payroll to feel as if they owed her. She wasn't one of those bosses. Stuart, yes. He sent his assistant on tons of errands and conveniently forgot to reimburse her for one thing or another. They fought about that all the time, but he never relented.

"Then add it to my paycheck, ma'am."

"I would rather give you the cash back." She dug her hand in the bakery bag and pulled out a light-brown muffin stuffed with goodness. Her nose filled with the sweet scents of banana and blueberry.

"Is this a blueberry banana oatmeal muffin?"

"Yes, ma'am."

"Please stop calling me ma'am. I'm sorry I bit your head off. You don't have to be so formal because of it. How did you know?" She held up the muffin. This was her favorite muffin, and she had it for breakfast whenever she had time to bake. Even Stuart didn't know this was her favorite.

The corner of his mouth twitched under his mustache and beard. "I watched your television show to help me with the assignment. You talked about that thing in almost every episode."

"I did not." Had she?

"You did. Every single one except for the time you renovated a house owned by a baker who made you chocolate chip. Do you plan on sitting a while? I can wait up at the top of the dock for you." He turned to go.

"Reade?"

"Yes?"

"Why did you do something so nice for me?"

"You're making a big deal out of nothing. It's a muffin."

She supposed he was right. She couldn't remember the last time someone other than her father had been so thoughtful, though. She loved renovating houses, but it was always the needs of the homeowners ahead of hers, and the needs of the network executives ahead of hers, and Stuart always put his needs ahead of hers too.

She swiped at the moisture building in the corner of her eyes. How pathetic to cry over something as mundane as a muffin.

"Would you mind staying on the dock with me?" She grabbed a seat on the bench that faced the water and hoped he would sit with her. His nearby presence would be more comforting than having him fifty feet away. Maybe it was his size next to her that brought a sense of comfort. Like a big security blanket.

"As you wish." He turned his back to the lake.

"Don't you want to sit?"

"I'd rather keep watch." He left her to her muffin.

"Would you like some?" She tore the muffin in half and held out a piece. He shook his head. "You're a man of few words."

"You aren't paying me to talk."

She nibbled at the muffin and drank her coffee, wanting to break the silence with talk of anything, but Reade's squared shoulders and ramrod straight back made her close her mouth each time. The remainder of the muffin dried up in her mouth. She wanted someone to talk to that wasn't her father. All her close friends dropped off one by one when she didn't have time for their calls or visits. She had been so caught up in her own life, she'd forgotten to treat her relationships with kindness. She tossed what was left of the muffin into the lake and wiped her hands on her jeans. She itched to keep moving and marched past him.

"Change of mind?" He followed behind her.

"I want to circle halfway around the lake then back. I have energy to burn. Fresh air does that to me." And the brush-off from her bodyguard. He wasn't supposed to be her friend, but they were going to be spending a lot of time together. It was in their best interest to get along. Couldn't he see that?

"It's going to be hot soon. The dry air will dehydrate you, and we don't have water. Are you sure you want to walk that far today?"

"We're by a lake. How dry can the air be?" She made her way through sandy patches on the lake's edge.

"We're on the west side of Montana. The air is dry here unlike the east side that gets its weather from the Atlantic. We should have hydration for a full hike. We're going to have to turn around sooner than you'd like."

"I thought I wasn't paying you to talk." The ground dipped with almost every step as she followed the border of the lake. She had expected flatter land this close to the water.

"You are paying me to keep you safe."

She walked right into that one. "Safe from my stalker."

"I wouldn't be doing my job if I allowed you to end up in the hospital under any circumstance. My boss would fire me on the spot and with good reason." He caught up to her with those long legs. He met her step for step with barely a deep breath.

Sweat broke out on her neck as she marched on. Her lungs worked hard as she covered more ground. She could demolish a wall by hand. She should certainly be able to navigate this uneven terrain with less difficulty.

"Bebe, you're not answering. Is it because you're out of breath? Maybe you should stop."

"I don't need to stop. But since you're being so insistent, we'll go back sooner. I wouldn't want you to get in trouble with your boss." She could use some water, but she would not tell him he was right.

The smug look on his hairy face was enough to make her sweat more. She opened her mouth to tell him not to enjoy himself so much when the ground crumpled. Her leg dropped into a hole, and she tilted like a cut tree and fell on her side. Her ankle screamed out in pain and so did she.

CHAPTER 6

READE BIT BACK A CURSE. That stubborn woman couldn't sit still on her dock and enjoy the damn breakfast he brought her. She had to get herself all riled up because he didn't want to gossip like a hen, and now she'd gone and probably sprained her ankle.

"Sit tight." He helped her lean against a tree. He was going to need to get a good look at it.

"It hurts." She winced as she moved her leg.

"Don't try to put pressure on it. I'm going to have to take off your shoe." Advanced notice was called for in a situation like this. If she had been one of his men injured on duty, he would've yanked the boot off right in that hole.

But she was small compared to him, and he didn't want to hurt her any more than she was. He also didn't want her to haul off and slug him.

Her calf muscle was strong under his touch. He

47

expected that after he eyed up her legs last night, but he didn't expect to feel his low belly tighten when she flexed against his fingers.

"Nice and easy." He worked the boot over her heel and peeled off her sock. Her pink painted toenails wiggled at him.

She dug her fingernails into his shoulder. "Is it broken?"

He wanted to meet her gaze, but she had scrunched her eyes closed. A smile tugged on his lips, but he forced it away. "It's not broken."

Her eyes flew open. "It's not?"

"You've never broken a bone before." It wasn't a question. If she had, she would've known whatever she was facing wasn't that. Moving those toes would've been pretty hard too. He didn't know how a house renovator hadn't at least broken a finger.

"Lucky, I guess," she said as if she had read his thoughts.

"You're damn lucky since you've been shot. If that bullet had hit bone, you would've broken it."

"Reade, please. I'm going to puke as it is. Tell me. Is it bad?"

"You've got some swelling here." He pointed to the side of her ankle that was getting bigger by the second. "Maybe a sprain. Maybe not. You're going to need to ice it and keep it up."

"Let me see." She pushed his hand away to get a better look. Her touch sent a small current up his arm to his chest. It had been far too long since he'd been in a woman's company.

He had stopped the one-night stands a while ago. In the morning, he had wanted more than empty promises, but he had never wanted to make the commitment. He still didn't. Not with this beautiful woman or any other. But Bebe Murano had him thinking about some meaningless sex.

"I have plans to work on the cabin," she said, dragging his attention away from the tingling sensation roaming over his skin.

"Not for a few days. I'll help you stand." He took in the full view of her. Her dark curls sprung out from that ring holding her hair back. She worked her bottom lip under her teeth every time she shifted. She had dirt on her pants. Anyone with half a brain would find her beautiful.

"Wait." She put her hand up.

"I promise you won't get hurt. You can lean on me."

"Lean on you?"

"Or I can carry you back."

"Definitely not that. How do we do this?"

He squatted beside her good side. "Put your arm around my shoulder until you're standing. I think after that you'll have to wrap your arm around my waist because of the height difference."

She leaned her soft curves into him as he helped her get upright. Her body fit snug against his. For once he wished the details didn't light up inside his head nonstop. In the Rangers, and on this job, details saved lives, but paying attention to the nuances of a pretty lady only meant trouble.

"Is this okay?" She held his gaze.

He cleared his throat and tried to ignore the heat coming off her. "As long as it is for you. Let's try to walk."

They hopped along for a little while. She grunted as they navigated the way back, but she never complained. Her grip around his waist was strong, but she leaned more and more into him with each tortured step.

"Stop," he said.

"I can do it." She huffed and puffed and wiped the sweat from her brow.

"I don't doubt you're determined if you have to crawl the rest of the way. But I think your nails have drawn blood from digging into my side. Not that I mind, but this is my favorite t-shirt, and I don't want it stained."

A small chuckle escaped from her lips. She dipped her head forward. Her hair fell over her face. He brushed it back to find her smiling.

"I'm sorry." She leaned her head against his shoulder. "This isn't as easy as I thought, and you were right about the day getting hotter. Can we take a break?"

"How about this?" He scooped her up in his arms.

She squealed. "Reade, put me down."

"I can carry you in a fraction of the time. You need that ankle on ice. Deal with it." And he needed to put a little space between them. Carrying her was the fastest way to stop touching her.

He hadn't responded so quickly to a woman in ages. If he tried to think back on the last time, he would say it had to be when he met Jennifer while he was still a young man who believed all things were possible. Like love. He had thought he and Jennifer were a lot alike, but they were too different. She figured it out before he did and when he was on a tour. She didn't want to be married to the military. Or him.

By the time he and Bebe returned to the cabin, he was drenched in sweat. He deposited her in the Adirondack chair on the porch. "You okay?" He used the bottom of his shirt to wipe his face.

She stared up at him with wide eyes. "Um, yes, thanks."

Did her ankle hurt more than she was letting on? He hoped it was only a small sprain that a little ibuprofen would handle. He'd hate to have to bring her to the emergency room. Most likely they'd be safe, but she was a celebrity. Her presence would draw too much attention at a place like a hospital. With everyone snapping pictures and taking videos, her location could end up on the web in seconds. If he had to, he'd call Linc and see if there was a doctor who made house calls.

"I'll go inside first. I prefer to check the residence each time before we reenter. Let me have the key." He held out his hand.

"I didn't bring it. I was so mad at you I forgot to even lock the door."

"Well, shit." He ran a hand over the top of his head. "Keep quiet."

He lifted her out of the chair and helped her lean against the side of the house away from the door. A quick visual search of the outside area didn't indicate anyone had been around, but he would've preferred the ground to be muddy so he could see footprints.

He withdrew his gun from his ankle holster.

"Is that really necessary?"

He put his fingers to his lips. He could be overreacting, but it was his job to be cautious. Better safe than sorry as they said. He wasn't one to take risks when it came to saving lives.

He pushed the door open with his fingers. The front room looked as they had left it. He went down the small hall to her bedroom.

And froze.

CHAPTER 7

BEBE WANTED TO THROW UP. The pain in her ankle turned her stomach. She had fought the retching the entire way back from the lake. Leaning against the house, out of sight of trouble but with time to think about her mistake made the bile burn her throat. She had been stupid to leave the door unlocked. She had put herself and Reade in harm's way. If she could walk, she would march right into the cabin and help him face whatever she may have caused.

"Reade?" He had told her to stay quiet, but the not knowing made her crazy.

He appeared in the doorway. The narrowed eyes, the pressed lips, and the fact he couldn't meet her gaze made her knees give way. She slid down the side of the house.

"What happened?" Her voice wobbled out of her mouth like a table on three legs.

He kicked the doorframe but didn't answer her.

"Damn it, Reade. Say something."

"I need you to come with me." He held out his hand and helped her to her feet.

"You're scaring me."

He gripped both of her hands in his. "I need you to trust me."

"Is there a reason I wouldn't?" She didn't understand what he was trying to say and wanted whatever was happening to be over.

He put his arm around her waist and pulled her against his strong body. If she wasn't scared for her life, she might enjoy the strength that rolled off those muscles.

He stopped outside the bedroom door. "Brace yourself."

Her heart picked up speed. She wanted to yell to stop. That she didn't need to see whatever he was about to show her. They could go back outside and forget what was behind the door. She tried to suck in air, but her lungs didn't seem to work.

"Is he inside that door?" Had Benjamin Morris hung himself in her bedroom?

Reade pushed the door open and caught her before she hit the floor.

"Come on," he said, turning her away from the room.

"No. I need a better look." She pushed away from

him and hopped on her good foot a couple of feet closer to the bed.

Every inch of the quilt was covered with black-and-white photos of her. Some of the photos were duplicates, but each one caught her from a distance, completely unaware she was being watched. Photos of her getting into her car in California. Of her walking inside the airport. Photos of her coming out of the coffee shop and the general store here in Montana. More photos of her at the hardware store the day Reade arrived. And one photo taken of her from outside the kitchen window of this very cabin. She had a mug in her hand and wore her robe. Every photo had a red X through her face.

She leaned forward, balancing on one foot, to grab a picture.

"Don't touch those. It's a crime scene."

"A crime scene? You said he couldn't find me. You said I would be safe. You made it sound as if this job was a no-brainer because you had checked it out, and I had hidden this cabin well. You lied." She dug her nails into her palms to keep her hands from doing anything else like hitting him or shoving all those pictures off the bed.

She wanted to set the bed on fire. She'd never be able to stay here. All her plans to come to Montana to heal and start over were gone. Washed away like dirt on her boots. This land was supposed to be her sanctuary, and she had foolishly believed Reade could keep her safe.

Her ankle throbbed, and her supporting leg begged for her to get off it, but she stood her ground because she wanted Reade to argue with her. She hoped he would dare to say he hadn't promised anything just so she could scratch his eyes out.

"I'm sorry. I thought you had covered your tracks. I didn't know how determined this guy was."

"Shouldn't it have been your job to know?"

"Yes." He ran a hand over his head.

She wasn't expecting him to agree. In fact, she couldn't stay mad at him if he did, and she needed to have someone to direct her anger at. Stuart had never stayed in the room when she got mad, and his dismissal only made her madder. She often ran after him and forced him to confront her. He never acquiesced. Benjamin Morris tormented her from afar. She wanted to confront him too. But there Reade stood with as much confusion on his face as she had racing through her blood.

"I need to sit down." She pushed past him and made her way into the living area. The small space closed in on her. Once nightfall came, she would be trapped.

"I can't stay here. What am I going to do?" The tears burned her eyes, but she forced them back.

Reade came into the room. "I need to make a call,

then we'll get you settled. Why don't you sit and put your leg on the table?" He pulled out his phone and tapped the screen, not waiting for her to respond. "Linc, we've got a big problem. Someone broke in. I need you here fast."

"No police," she said.

"No official police. Yeah, thanks." He ended the call and shoved the phone in his pocket. "It's a bad idea to keep the police out. They can look for the guy too."

"If the police tell anyone about this, it could be all over the news. I don't want the whole world to know he found me."

"Maybe if the whole world knows, then we can find him faster. He won't be able to hide."

"Won't it give him exactly what he wants?"

"You mean the attention. Bebe, I'm sorry if I led you to believe you'd never have to worry about him again. I did think of this job more as a babysitting assignment, and that was wrong. It's my fault he got inside. Not yours. I'll ask Linc to assign someone else for you. I'm going to check out the rest of the property and my cabin. Stay put." He went out the door and locked it from the outside.

She leaned back into the corner of the couch and pulled a throw pillow over her chest. Her mind couldn't stay away from those photos left to torment her. Benjamin Morris had been in this house. His presence haunted the whole place. He wouldn't stop until he caught her. Maybe the gunshot had been for Stuart, but in the end, Morris wanted her dead in the name of love.

And no one could keep her safe.

CHAPTER 8

READE THREW the rest of his belongings into his duffel. In less than forty-eight hours, he had screwed up worse than any other time in his life. He had been a razor-sharp Ranger, but since he'd been home, he'd grown soft. Bebe could've been hurt because of him. Or worse.

As soon as Linc was done speaking with Bebe, he would head out. Linc and Bebe sat in the living area of Reade's cabin talking about the case. Linc was trying to convince her to bring in the locals, but she wouldn't hear of it.

He wiped a hand across to the top of his head. Linc was probably going to fire him so that meant he'd have to go back to working construction. That was fine by him. He didn't have to talk much to the other guys. He did as he was told, and when the job was done, he moved on.

The bodyguard job required him to get to know his subject. He had accomplished more than just watching Bebe's show. He had learned everything he could about her, and the more he learned, the more he wanted to know. That was dangerous business.

He tugged on the zipper of his duffel until the bag finally closed. The bedroom door rolled to the side. It was one of those barn door things used to save space. He'd learned about that from watching Bebe's show too. She liked to use that design as much as she liked those muffins.

Linc stood in the doorway. His eyes were hooded. He pinched the bridge of his nose. "Let's take a walk," he said.

"Yes, sir."

"I'm not sir out here. Just Lincoln." Linc didn't wait for him but headed out the front door.

He hurried past Bebe sitting in the chair with her leg raised and a bag of ice on her ankle. She didn't look up from her phone when he passed. He couldn't blame her. She had hired him to do a job that he couldn't do. She must be terrified after seeing those photos. He hadn't wanted to show her, knowing it would make her upset, but she also needed to know what was happening in order to stay aware.

The afternoon sun cooked everything under its touch. The heat rolled off the ground even with a slight breeze pushing through the evergreens. This property should have brought her some peace and quiet. It would've for him in another time. He shielded his eyes to get a better look at Lincoln glaring at him.

"I bagged all the photos and dusted for prints." Linc fisted his hands on his hips. "I don't think we'll find anything unusual there. Morris has made it clear what he wants even before now. He probably didn't try to hide the fact he touched them. I'm giving all the evidence to Hank so we can continue to build a case since Bebe doesn't want the locals involved. We're going to catch this guy."

"I don't understand why the security camera didn't notify me when he approached the cabin." He had been racking his brain over that one, even checked the app a few dozen times. He had tested those damn cameras himself, and they had worked fine.

"I can only speculate on how he dodged the security system. Doesn't matter how he did it. He got past them. I'm just glad she wasn't in the house alone when he showed up," Linc said.

The idea of her being vulnerable to the likes of a sick, twisted bastard like Morris made his blood burn hotter than the sun. A man who tried to shoot someone in the name of love, or stalked them to get attention, was out of his mind. No one should be subjected to that terror, and he wanted to keep Bebe safe. She deserved that much after what she'd been through.

"She can't be left alone even for a minute. Whoever you put on her now has to know that." He didn't like the idea of someone else watching her. He wanted to be the one in charge of her safety. But after today, maybe she'd be better off without him on the case. She couldn't trust him, and having that trust was important to her.

"Are you quitting on me?" Linc narrowed his eyes and set his jaw. His body shifted slightly, but Reade caught it. Linc took a ready stance.

He threw his hands up. "You can't want me on this any longer."

"Why not?"

"Because I let that asshole get past me. I'd sure as hell fire my ass." He would've done it on the phone. No man under his command had screwed up the way Reade had today.

Linc shook his head. "Man, you haven't changed. Give yourself a break. My guess is Morris waited until you were gone before going inside. He left those photos to scare her but nothing more."

Nothing more for now. "This will escalate."

"It could, but that's not this stalker's motivation. He thinks she wants to be with him. He's misinterpreted her social media, even things she's said on her show. He told all that to the arresting officers."

"It was still my fault that I didn't double-check the door was locked." That had been a rookie mistake, and he hadn't been a rookie in twenty years, but she had fired him up with her accusations. A woman who knew herself and didn't take his crap had a way of reaching places he thought he'd locked up tight.

"He would've found a way in. He's determined if nothing else. What I need to know is how did he know she was here, and where is he now?" Linc scratched at his chin.

"She might've told someone where she was going. One of those online media outlets that hawk celebrities could've followed her too and posted her getting on a plane to Montana." He would also make a call to that ex-husband of hers and find out what he knew. The asshat hadn't called her once to see how she was doing.

"Maybe. I'll scour the internet to see what I find. In the meantime, go inside and keep her company. She needs you."

"She can't stay here." The place had been compromised, and he had done a lousy job of protecting her.

"This is exactly where she stays. Morris has already proven he can find her. There's no point in wasting resources to find another place. I'm going to give you extra men to keep watch. A car at the foot of the drive. Men around the clock out here. You inside with her until we find the guy."

"She isn't going to want me here."

"She asked that I not fire you. Not that I planned on doing that. She pled your case. Said it was all her fault that door wasn't locked. That you'd done nothing but your job including staying up all night and bringing her breakfast."

"She said that?"

"She likes you." Linc patted him on the shoulder. "Just don't get involved with a client while you're on the job. I've had too many men do that. It's bound to backfire one of these days."

"Too many men including you." Reade knew the story of Linc protecting his old girlfriend when a Santa Claus blew up her Christmas party. Now Linc was happily married to his former client.

"I don't count. I loved Serra long before I started this job."

He took a quick glance at the cabin. Bebe wanted him to stay on. He shouldn't read too much into that or what Linc just said. Bebe was used to him, that's all. She probably didn't want to get to know another guard after this. The devil she knew, and all.

"What do I say to her?" He should apologize again. And thank her for asking that he stay. Other than that, Linc had to be wrong about her feeling anything more than gratitude. She liked that he brought her that muffin. She liked that he was there when she fell. The rest she didn't like at all. And would probably hate once she got to know him.

"Just do your job. Worry about getting laid later."

"Whoa. I don't want to have sex with her." She was beautiful and desirable. If he had met her at a bar, and she wasn't some famous person with a television show, he might ask her to dance or have a beer with him. He could watch her eyes light up all day when she smiled, but a woman like Bebe wouldn't want a simple former Ranger like him with nothing to offer.

"Yeah, well, I think she wants you too."

"She did not say that." He rubbed his hand across the top of his head. It might've been nicer if she mentioned that to him and not Linc. And then what would she really want with him? Linc had to be wrong.

Linc barked out a laugh. "She didn't say a word about wanting to get in your pants. But I can still tell when a woman is hot for a man."

"But I just met her." Like that mattered. He had had one-night stands before based on nothing more than a strong physical response to one another. Bebe didn't seem like the kind of woman satisfied by one night. He didn't think he would be either where she was concerned. He didn't know her well, except what he learned for the case, but she had a depth to her.

"Must be that beard. Your backup will be here within the hour. They'll check in with you. Until then, I'll sit at the road. I'll be in touch with whatever else I find out about Benjamin Morris."

He waited until Linc pulled down the driveway before turning for the cabin.

He didn't want to go back in there.

She scared the hell out of him.

CHAPTER 9

BEBE ENDED THE CALL. Now was the worst possible time for that invitation to come in. Never mind that she probably sprained her ankle and had refused a doctor's care which would mean it would take longer to heal, but after today, she couldn't get in front of a camera ever again.

For a brief moment, she thought she might be able to return to work, but that moment was over. The next phone call would be to her agent. She would sign the rights of the show over to Stuart. He could have it all. She didn't want anyone to know her ever again.

Reade came through the front door. He narrowed his eyes and crossed his arms over his chest.

"What?" She had to drag her gaze away. She would never be able to get the image of his muscular abs out of her mind. He had lifted his shirt to wipe his face without a thought, but now she had thoughts better left untouched.

"Thank you." It came out as a growl.

"Thank you?" She wasn't expecting that.

"That's what I said. Thank you for, you know, talking to Linc." He waved his hand in the air.

"You didn't do anything wrong. If you wanted off the case because I have refused to listen to you, I would understand. I haven't been the most cooperative client." She hoped he wouldn't go, but she hadn't missed how he had packed his things. She could try to persuade him, but Reade seemed like the kind of man who made up his mind and that was the end of the discussion.

He scratched the top of his head. "You can stay here if you don't want to go back to your cabin."

"When will Lincoln have the new bodyguard? Maybe I could find a hotel or something." She didn't want to be cramped in this cabin with a stranger, which looked like she would be. She barely knew Reade, but he had been attentive to her needs so far. That gave her confidence in him. And she liked the way he smelled.

"I'm staying and so are you. Linc doesn't want to move you. There's no point really. You'll have extra protection here. Linc gave all the physical evidence to our boss. The Brotherhood will be looking into your stalker. No police, like you asked."

He was staying. She closed her eyes and let out a

long breath. And he had respected her wishes of no police.

"Are you okay?" He sat beside her on the couch. Their thighs touched. His was large and solid. Strong like him.

He smelled like the outdoors. Her fingers wanted to run over his beard and find out if it was soft. She clasped her hands in her lap instead. This man had her thinking things she had no business entertaining. They hardly knew each other, yet she wanted to know more.

"I'm fine. Thanks, but would it be okay if we slept here tonight instead of my cabin? I'm not sure if I'll be able to sleep in that bed ever again." She might want to demolish the entire cabin and rebuild it before stepping foot back inside.

"You can have the bed. I'll take the couch."

"How am I going to feel whole again? Morris took something from me when he left those pictures. Breaking into my house and then following me with the camera hurts worse than the gunshot did."

The violation had stripped her of any emotional protection she had built up. Her nerves were scraped raw. Fear darkened the corners of her life like growing mold because some stranger thought he had a right to her and her attention.

Reade gripped her knee. "Hey, it's going to be okay. It doesn't feel that way now, but it will once he's caught and put behind bars for good now. Hank

Patterson and Lincoln Smith are the very best. They won't make any mistakes."

"How will I feel safe even if he's behind bars?" Tears filled her eyes, making his face blurry.

"I'll keep you safe. I promise I won't let anything happen to you. Ever."

"That's a pretty big promise." One he couldn't possibly fulfill even if she wanted him to.

Which she did.

ONCE BEBE MADE THE CALL, there was no going back. She could not undo this so she had to be sure. She dropped the phone on the bed and limped out to the main area. The swelling had gone down on her ankle. She could even put some pressure on it. She had probably just twisted it. For once, luck was on her side. Actually, she'd been lucky a lot in her life at least in the career area. Her intimate relationship problems had nothing to do with bad fortune. She hadn't been smart enough to pick the right guy.

The aroma of tomato sauce filled the small space. Reade stood at the stove with his back to her. He stirred a wooden spoon inside a big pot and whistled a tune she didn't recognize. She took the opportunity to admire his broad shoulders and narrow waist. His jeans hugged his tight butt and long legs. She shouldn't bother to notice the nice things about

Reade. Her luck was running out, and she didn't trust herself to know when a man was right for her.

"Something smells good," she said.

He turned at the sound of her voice.

"You need to get off that foot." He went back to his task.

She slid onto the kitchen chair and propped her foot up on the one opposite. The vantage point also continued to give her a reason to watch Reade. "It doesn't hurt as much. Have the other men arrived?" She wanted Reade to have help if he needed it tonight. Morris could return. Reade had to sleep at some point. He could be tired and miss something important. She was no help to him in her condition.

The sun was close to setting. Dusk set her nerves on edge. She was grateful for the long summer days. This whole mess during the short days of winter would be far worse. She resisted the urge to get back up and check the locks, but her fingers prickled to test them one by one.

"Everyone is stationed in their places. We're safe. Benjamin Morris won't come back here tonight. Linc has men searching for him. They'll find him soon." He cast a genuine smile that lit up his eyes. "You won't need me much longer."

A yummy warmth spread over her, gluing her gaze to his. Who was this man that had walked into her life a short time ago but had her remembering how nice a man's touch could be?

He poured pasta into a large bowl and broke the connection. Or it was her skittish nerves misinterpreting the chemistry in the room. That had to be it. Reade wouldn't be interested in her. She was a mess and a celebrity which he had made perfectly clear he wouldn't want to be a part of.

"But you'll stay on as long as I want, right?"

"I guess that's up to Lincoln. He's the boss." Reade pulled bread out of the oven and cut it into small strips.

"But if I pay? I mean my money has to be able to give me what I'm asking for. If my television show is the reason I'm in this mess, the money has to be the upside, or I've done all of this for nothing." Fear made her mouth run off. What she had said wasn't true at all. The money was nice and helped her dad, but she would reno houses and decorate them for free if she could. She wanted to help people live in nice places. Places they would be glad to come home to. For some people, that meant places that were safe.

He narrowed his eyes. "You're the client. I'm sure your money will get you what you want."

"I just meant if I didn't feel comfortable on my own." She wasn't explaining this correctly. The cold stare in his eyes said he misunderstood. He obviously didn't know the kind of paralysis she felt because of this stalker. A man like Reade wouldn't allow fear to stop him from doing anything.

"You can pay for whatever you want. Money buys

it all, doesn't it? You can pay for round-the-clock security. You can probably pay for me to stand on my head all night too."

"Reade, I didn't—"

"You're used to getting your way. I get it. People like you always have someone ready to jump at your every wish. Isn't there some urban legend about only brown M&Ms allowed in a dressing room? Why wouldn't you expect to have a bodyguard for as long as you wanted? We're for hire, aren't we?" He dumped pasta onto plates. Sauce spilled on the counter.

"What do you mean people like me?"

"Celebrities. Famous people. You snap your fingers and everyone jumps. Did your husband stop doing your bidding? Is that why you left him?" He tossed the wooden spoon into the bowl and scratched the top of his head.

"For a second, I thought you were a decent guy. Different from other men, but I was wrong. You're a big ass like the rest of them." She pushed out of the chair and tripped over the table leg. She went straight down on her hip and smacked her bad ankle in the process. She bit back a curse.

He dropped to her side. "Are you okay?"

She pushed his hands away. "Leave me alone." The damn tears threatened to come. She closed her eyes and took a deep breath, hoping to keep them at bay.

"Let me help you." He gripped her elbows to ease her up.

She leaned her weight into him just long enough to stand. Then she would attempt to march away as best she could with some semblance of dignity. She'd lock herself in the bedroom all night and not eat his food.

He didn't ease up on his grip as she balanced on her good leg. She stared up at him, ready to pounce, but the softness in his eyes froze the words in her mouth.

"Did you get hurt?" His words floated out on a whisper.

The heat rolled off him mixed with his woodsy scent and clung to her. The inches between them were filled with an electric current, at least for her. She had to be wrong, believing an attraction existed between them.

"I'm not hurt." Only her pride and her ego.

"I'm sorry for what I just said about you. Sometimes I shoot my mouth off without thinking." He kept his grip on her. His voice took on a husky quality that made heat fill her low belly.

"Why do you think my job is so bad?" She didn't move. She didn't want to break the connection.

"Fixing houses is great. It's the other part that I don't like." He brushed a piece of hair from her face. "What you do makes you vulnerable."

"It's the price I'm willing to pay." At least she used

to be willing to give up her privacy. She had never dreamed something like Benjamin Morris would happen to her. Even though she came into millions of people's homes once a week, she was still just Benedetta Murano, the girl whose mother died in a drive-by shooting, the girl who liked to play with hammers instead of dolls. She never fit in growing up. Everyone looked at her out of the corner of their eye, afraid to say the wrong thing to the misfit with no mother.

"I don't think anyone should give up their privacy the way celebrities do, but you… You're different to me. You're special. If you were my woman, I would want you safe…safe, protected, and not exposed for someone to take advantage of."

"I'm not special." She eased away from him because that statement about being his woman made the heat in her belly burn hotter. A woman of Reade's would never have to worry about being safe or taken care of. Stuart never tried to protect her. He hadn't even paid attention when Morris first started sending the aggressive emails.

"You're wrong. You're generous and kind."

"How do you know that? We just met." She dropped onto the couch. Her ankle hurt from the recent spill, and her head couldn't process what he had said.

"I know about the single mother you helped. The one that didn't end up on television. She had left her abusive husband and started over, but the house she had bought was a mess. The previous owner wouldn't make good. You flew in with a skeleton crew and worked nonstop to make her space livable. You called in favors. That was a very generous thing to do." He came over to the couch and sat beside her, using up all the oxygen in the little space.

She needed air or to finally find out if that beard was soft. "Anyone would've done what I did. That woman needed help."

Lily had been on the run from her ex-husband for a long time. She had done everything by the letter of the law to get away from him. The night before she moved into that house, which was nothing more than a foundation and walls covered in mold, her ex came to her apartment and forced his way in. He had attacked her, but she called the police, and he was arrested. She never wanted him to win. Lily's bravery made fixing houses look like a waste of time.

"And you helped her. You could've ignored her request, but you didn't." He eased her leg onto the coffee table. "Keep it elevated."

His large hands swallowed her calf. Her mind wandered to the idea of those hands moving else-where. Her pant leg had shifted, and the touch of his skin against hers sent shivers over her body.

"Where did you get that information? We kept it out of the press to keep her privacy safe. The network didn't even know about it. Stuart didn't even know the whole story."

"The Brotherhood can dig up anything, and I want to know every detail about an assignment. I don't leave any stone unturned. Trust me when I say you're special, and I'll stop shooting my mouth off about your job." He pushed off the couch, but she placed a hand on his thigh to stop him.

"You are a sweet man."

He brushed a piece of her hair away from her face again. "I'm not sure what's happening here, but I have a job to do, and I need to stay focused. You could easily become a distraction."

"I don't want to distract you, but I think I want to kiss you." She resisted the embarrassment, wanting to turn her gaze away. She had never been so forward with a man in her life.

"I believe kissing a client is against company policy." He leaned in closer.

"After all that yelling at me about needing to get my way, it looks like I might have to fire you after all." She inched in too.

"Does that mean you really want to kiss me?" His voice was soft and low.

"I believe it does."

He eased in more, taking his time. She wanted to pull him to her and hurry this along, but waiting was like ringing the last drop of goodness out. Her skin tingled with the anticipation of his lips meeting hers.

Her heart played a quick rhythm against her ribs. She licked her bottom lip.

A ringing from the other room broke the current between them and sent her reeling. He sat back and blinked.

"What is that?" He searched for the origin of the sound.

"It's my phone. I left it on the bed." And since the cabin wasn't much bigger than a three-car garage, the bedroom was close enough the phone could be heard. And ruin the mood.

"I'll grab it for you." He hurried away and returned as quickly.

The screen read Stuart's name. This was the call she had been avoiding. Reade went back to the dinner that was probably cold and congealed by now.

"Aren't you going to answer that?" he said.

She glanced at him and then the phone.

She was out of time.

CHAPTER 10

READE CIRCLED the cabin a final time. The sky was filled with stars. Frogs jumped and croaked in the lake. A set of wind chimes played music in the breeze. Everything was in place. Jax Montero sat watch at the end of the driveway. He'd be there all night. Standing guard at the cabin were two new guys on his team, Mason Fox and Boone Carter. A fourth man would round out Linc's new close protection team, but that guy wasn't on duty. They would have to learn to work together. He wasn't worried about that. They would either get along, or they would have to stay out of his way.

What he was worried about was going back inside that cabin and facing Bebe. He had been a damn fool, wanting to kiss her. He'd never been so grateful to be saved by the bell. He could jeopardize their safety if he even let his guard down for a moment. When this was over, if she was still interested and not deterred by the mundane of real life, he would ask her out on a proper date.

A date. What was he thinking? A woman like her would not be interested in his boring life, and he was done dating. Dating could lead to more. He wasn't in the market for more. He wanted to keep moving. Settling down would choke the life from him.

He gave a quick nod to Fox and Carter before settling inside. He kicked off his boots and placed them beside the woodburning stove that had been lit. The curtains on the window had been drawn and clipped together with clothespins.

The bedroom door was half open. Bebe's long legs were visible on the bed. She had changed into shorts. Her calf muscles flexed as she wiggled her toes. Something in his belly twisted. His fingers craved the feel of her leg again. When he had touched her earlier, the shock to his skin had run straight to his chest.

"Everything looks good outside. You have nothing to worry about. Get some sleep." He leaned against the doorjamb, trying to keep a safe distance.

She eyed him over her black glasses perched at the end of her cute nose. She had wrapped a blanket around her shoulders and held a book in her hand. "Thanks, but I don't know if I can sleep." She held up the book. The cover looked like a thriller novel. Something he would read.

"Did everything work out on your phone call?" He didn't want to go away just yet. She might be cold under that blanket, and if invited he would gladly climb under it and keep her warm, but he guessed the blanket was more of a shield. Probably from what happened earlier with that near kiss.

"Stuart wants me to come back to work. We have an opportunity to do some good and make him a bundle." She removed the glasses and closed the book.

"Aren't you going to make money too?" He shifted against the molding, trying to find a comfortable spot. After hours on his feet, his back acted up.

"I don't care about the money. I care about the project."

"Did you say you would go back to work?" That was where she belonged, not here with him. The pain climbed up his back into his shoulders. He rolled his head on his neck.

"Do you want to sit down? I can scoot over." She edged to the far side of the bed.

Like the room, the bed wasn't very big. If he stretched out in it, he'd probably take up all the space. Something Bebe might not appreciate, though he would enjoy having her close and inhaling her sexy scent.

"I'm okay right here. Well, what did you say to Stuart?" He tried to keep the sarcasm out of his voice as it drifted over the ex's name, but he failed.

She raised her eyebrows in acknowledgment of his tone of voice. Shit. He wasn't doing a very good job of hiding his feelings.

"I said I still don't know. I want to wait to decide until Benjamin Morris is caught for good, but part of me wonders if there won't be another Benjamin Morris standing in the wings to try and come after me. I want to renovate houses. I love my show, but I don't know what to do."

"What did your ex say to all that?"

She stared at her hands. "I told him I'd think about it and get back to him."

"So, you chickened out?" A smile tugged at his lips. He forced it back down. She hadn't come clean with old Stuart, but she had with him.

"Looks that way. I'm not brave. Like you." She held his gaze, and his belly twisted again.

He wasn't sure why it mattered that she thought he was brave. He'd been an Army Ranger for many years. He'd done plenty of things most people would never do. Some he was proud of, some not so much. He hadn't had the luxury of being paralyzed by fear. It didn't mean he wasn't scared shitless in war zones, but he had had a job to do. So, he did it. Every time. But to hear this beautiful, special woman say he was brave made his knees buckle.

"Don't kid yourself for a second. You're brave. Benjamin Morris gave you a lot to deal with, and you're handling it like a pro." He dropped onto the corner of the bed. She still had plenty of space, but he gave his legs and his back a break.

"All I want to do is hide. That's not brave."

"Making the smart decision can be braver than taking a risk."

She gave him a short laugh. "Nice try. But acting like a coward isn't the same thing as taking chances. People like you, or anyone that runs into danger, that's brave. Me, I'm running away from danger. That's why I came out to Montana. I ran away from life, from the public eye, from my mistakes."

"There's a difference between taking time to heal and jumping out of planes."

"You sound like you know that from experience."

"We've all had bad things happen in our lives. I'd better let you get some sleep. I'll be on the couch if you need me." He eased off the bed, wanting to put some space between the two of them before he lost all reason and removed that blanket from her shoulders and kissed the hell out of her.

"Reade?"

"Yeah?"

"Could you stay until I fall asleep? I know it sounds crazy and juvenile, but I would feel a lot better if you were in the room."

"The sofa is only two steps away." If the room had an extra chair, he'd be glad to drop into it and wait until she was asleep, but he'd have to sit on the corner of this bed with her only inches away. His back begged for him to put his feet up. It would take nothing for him to cave and swing his legs up on the bed and lay beside her.

"Yeah, you're right. I'm being ridiculous." She reached for the lamp.

The blanket moved and showed more of her leg. She clicked the light and threw them into darkness except for the light of the moon streaming through the gauzy curtains.

He sat back down and wiped a hand over his face. "I'll stay until you fall asleep. Go on, now. Close your eyes." He could still make her out her shadow as she fluffed the pillow and turned onto her side.

He held his head in his hands. How the hell had he ended up in this situation? He thought this job would've been a piece of cake. Now he was turned all around and the stalker was serious business. Instead of just babysitting her, he wanted to be out there looking for the lunatic, but Linc had given his orders. Reade was to stay back and watch Bebe. Hank Patterson was running the investigation piece. Benjamin Morris would make a mistake, and the Brotherhood Protectors would be ready.

Her hands touched his shoulders. He hadn't heard her move. Her touch was soft and cool. Her clean scent snuck around and knocked him in the head. He stifled a groan. Any other woman he would've made a move on with that kind of touch.

"Are you okay?" Her words didn't rise above a whisper. Her warm breath enticed him.

"Why wouldn't I be?"

"The heavy sighing." The heat from her body behind him rolled off her. Her hair fell on his shoulder and tickled his neck.

"I was doing that?" He hadn't noticed his breathing either because his mind had drifted away. Another mistake that could cost him.

"Yes." Her fingers kneaded his shoulders.

She had a lot of strength for a petite woman. Her hands dug into his tight muscles as they moved from his shoulders to his neck. He wanted to sigh with relief, but he bit his tongue.

He needed to stop this. Her touch caused madness. He wouldn't be able to hold off much longer, and especially not if those skilled hands went anywhere else. All he had wanted when he came inside was to keep a safe distance from the attraction, and he'd walked right into it.

Her fingers drifted back to his shoulders. He grabbed her hands.

"We can't do this." His voice sounded harsher than he meant.

She dropped back on the bed. "I'm sorry. You seemed so tense. I wanted to help you in some small way. You've been a big help to me."

"You hired me to help you." He certainly didn't

want her to think he was in over his head where her assignment was concerned.

"So?"

"It's my job to protect you and keep you safe. You are under no obligation to repay me." He had hoped, foolishly, that she might be as attracted as he was because of that almost kiss, but that didn't seem to be the case. He had misread her. He didn't usually have that problem with women. Or anyone, actually. Being able to read people made him good at what he did. When he did it. But she had him turned upside down.

"I wasn't being nice because I felt obligated."

"Then why?" He needed her to say it. She had to be the one to come forward first. He couldn't deny his attraction and didn't even want to. But this was his job, and his friend—his boss—was relying on him to follow the book. She had to want him because she couldn't deny the attraction between them either. Not because she pitied him.

"I wanted to make you feel better." Her words hung in the darkness.

"Bebe, there's too much at stake here. You need to say it. I promise you that you have nothing to fear with me, but you have to say it."

She pulled the blanket around her. He waited, while a current ran over his skin like heat lightning. He took another breath, but her silence made her wishes clear. He eased off the bed and tamped down the disappointment.

"Don't go."

"Why?"

"Because I want you in this bed."

CHAPTER 11

Bebe wanted to run. She had never been so forward with a man the way she was with Reade. She hardly knew him, but something about him made her want to do crazy things. It was his eyes. His eyes had given him away. And had given her the ounce of courage. Well, that and the dark. Here in this tiny bedroom, with Reade, she wasn't afraid of anything lurking in the shadows.

For the first time in her life, she felt safe. Reade had made that possible. Even with the recent breaking and entering, as long as Reade was with her, she would be able to get through this.

"Say something." Her dry throat strangled her voice.

Reade hadn't moved since she said she wanted him in bed. For a second, she thought she had misjudged what had been happening all day between them. Making a move on her bodyguard might be a bad idea because who knew how either of them would feel in the morning, but tonight she wanted to forget about logic and reason. She wanted to feel alive and not frightened. Reade's strong arms would give her that reprieve. What happened after would be on her.

He faced her. The light from the flames in the woodburning stove in the living area and the sliver of moonlight through the gauzy curtains helped her see his silhouette. He filled out the doorframe with his height and his broad shoulders.

"I want you to be sure. Because I'm sure, but if you aren't, I will walk away." His voice was soft but resolute. He gave a way out because he was a gentleman who lived by a code of honor.

"I'm sure."

"You can change your mind at any time." He eased closer to the bed.

His damn honor might kill the whole mood. "I don't want to think anymore. I want to feel."

"I can take care of that." He sat beside her and smoothed the hair away from her face.

His gentle touch made her tremble. He still smelled of the outdoors. She wanted more of his scent and unbuttoned his soft shirt with shaking fingers. She hoped he wanted her half as much as she wanted this to happen.

She brushed the shirt away from his shoulders.

She took a second to admire his sculpted muscles. Her lips found the soft spot between his collarbones while her hands traced the lines and angles of his chest and abdomen. Her fingers lingered on the soft down of his chest hair.

He ran his hands over her arms then he used his warm knuckle to tilt up her chin. "I want to see your face before I kiss you," he said.

"Do you like what you see?"

"Very much."

His lips pressed against hers, but she couldn't wait. She opened her mouth to allow him inside. His tongue swept around hers, making heat burn in her core. She wished his hair was long enough to tangle her fingers in. Instead, she wrapped her hand around his neck to bring him closer.

Pressed against his powerful chest, with their tongues exploring and probing, she needed more. Her clothes were in the way, but she didn't want to pull away from the kiss to remove them.

His hands moved over her body and caressed her legs. His fingers stopped right under the edge of her shorts. The blanket had slipped off at some point, but she wasn't cold or afraid.

She pressed him back against the pillows. The moonlight didn't give her enough light to enjoy the view completely. Her hands would have to tell her the whole story.

She made her living with her hands. They hadn't

let her down. She straddled him. The rough material of his jeans stretched by his erection rubbed her most sensitive spot and sent a current of electric energy through her body. She wriggled against him.

He moaned. The heat in her core turned up to a scorch at the power she held over him in that moment. Her fingers traced a line down his chest that her tongue followed. She wanted to taste all of him and fumbled with the button of his pants. She pushed them off his hips, and her tongue continued its exploration of his hip bones.

"Bebe, I won't last if you keep doing that." His voice was as rough as sandpaper.

She smiled but didn't remove her lips from their spot "I won't tell anyone the big, bad bodyguard had stamina control."

He gripped her shoulders and flipped her. She bounced on the bed, but laughter from both of them decorated the room in soft tones. He was above her, holding one hand over her head. He was fast and a solid mass of muscle who had trained to kill, but with her he was gentle and kind.

He kissed her nose. "Smart-ass."

"I like the way you respond to me." She wrapped her leg around his to get closer.

"Sweetheart, you haven't seen anything yet."

He brushed her hair away from her face again. His lips dropped to her neck. She tilted her head back to give him more space to leave his tender kisses. Each one made her toes curl.

He dragged her shirt over her head and tossed it. "Mmmm…. What a nice surprise. No bra." He took her breast in his mouth and teased her nipple into a hard stone.

She was glad she had discarded her bra before he came home. Her mind snagged on that last word. Thinking about Reade and a home was too much too soon. She forced the thought away and focused on the way he made her body come to life.

His hand found her leg again, but this time he pushed the edge of the shorts aside and gripped her bottom. She wrapped her leg around his thigh and pressed against him. She would explode if this went on much longer.

His tongue moved to her rib cage and then to her belly. He tugged off her shorts. She gave him a little help by lifting her hips. He continued his descent, leaving hot wet streaks with his lips and tongue until he was at her thigh.

Her breath came in fast bursts. Her heart couldn't keep up, and he hadn't even touched her in the spot that wanted him most. He positioned himself between her legs and brought his mouth down. His tongue and his touch sent her to the edge of frenzy until the desire inside her split wide open. She careened back to earth with pleasure.

"Wow." She covered her face with her hands.

"Glad you liked it." He slid off the bed and removed his jeans before climbing in next to her.

He gathered her close and kissed her. "All I want is to see that look on your face again."

Her body longed to be touched, and her breath had barely returned to normal. The ache between her legs begged for him to be inside her and grew more intense with each kiss he placed on her neck. Nothing would put an end to the need until he filled her up. "I want you."

"Are you certain? I can wait if you need more time." He caressed her cheek with a light touch.

"Please don't make me wait."

He pushed her legs apart and settled above her again. He held her gaze and paused outside her entrance before thrusting inside her. "You feel so good." He kissed her again hard and fast.

She sighed with ecstasy as he moved his hips. She raised her own hips to make room for all of him. She wanted the buildup of friction to go forever, but she needed to tumble off the edge of the cliff so much more.

Their frantic movements slicked their bodies with sweat. He reached between them and touched her where their bodies met. The sweet relief exploded through her.

He gripped her hip and pumped harder until his own release shook him. She wrapped her arms around him while he drifted back and his breath slowed.

"You make a man want to put down roots." He dropped his forehead to hers.

"That's the sex talking." She ran her fingers over his beard. Finally.

"You're very unexpected. I don't know what's going to happen, but if we're as good out of bed as we just were in bed, we'd be two lucky people." He brushed her hair away from her face.

"Can we curb the talk of a future for now? I just want to enjoy the humming in my body and you next to me." Her fingers continued to caress his beard.

"What's going on in that head of yours?" He eased off her and gathered her to him.

"My mind is empty after how well you played my body."

"The furrow of your brows and the clip in your voice you're trying to hide say different."

"Your attention to detail can be annoying." Though his attention to her body had been anything but.

"Spill it." He snuggled closer and ran his hands over her back.

In his arms, she could find the courage to tell him. "The special project Stuart wants us to do will air on several stations. If I do it, it's going to triple my popularity. I won't be able to go back to a private life for a long time."

"You're going to say yes" His hands stopped moving.

"I am." The decision had become clear when she told Reade he was brave. She wanted to be brave too for the woman who would need her help on this renovation.

He rolled onto his back and stared at the ceiling. "I think you're right. Let's talk about this another time."

"Reade, I'm sorry. I couldn't pass the chance up."

"What if we haven't captured Benjamin Morris again? Are you really willing to put your life on the line like that?"

"You'll have to keep me safe." She traced a circle on his pec muscle.

He gripped her hand. "The only way I can keep you safe is if you stay out of the spotlight until this is all over."

She flopped back on the bed and stared at the ceiling too. The inches between them seemed more like a chasm all of a sudden. "Then we have a problem on our hands."

"I believe we do."

CHAPTER 12

READE SLID OUT OF BED, trying not to disturb Bebe. She lay on her side with her back to him and took slow even breaths. She had been asleep for a while. He tried to succumb to a peaceful slumber while lying next to the beautiful woman who had rocked his world, but his mind churned with too many thoughts. He had never been much of a sleeper anyway. Usually, he left after sex with a woman, but this woman deserved better. He did want to stay, but he couldn't.

He shoved his legs into his jeans and padded out of the room, closing the door behind him. A little fresh air would do him good, maybe even give him the peace he needed so he could close his eyes for a few hours. His body begged his mind to shut up so he could recharge, but no go. He was in over his head with this lady.

He stepped out onto the back patio. It wasn't much more than a few large pavers arranged in a pattern, but it had an Adirondack chair that faced the mountains. He couldn't see them in the dark, but knowing they were there was enough. He could draw on their strength. The outdoors always brought him salvation. Working construction had always given him time outside. After this assignment, he had to go back. Lincoln had judged him wrong. Or he had misjudged himself.

The night air cooled his skin. He dropped down in the chair, taking the strain off his back that still ached.

"Hands in the air." A tall figure jumped around the corner of the house and pointed a gun at him.

"Easy, Mason. It's just me." He held his hands high. Getting shot right now would definitely suck.

"Sorry, man." Mason holstered his weapon at his hip. His white t-shirt did little to conceal the gun, which was fine by Reade. "I heard something and thought the worst. Everything okay?"

Mason Fox was also a former Army Ranger and had eyes like ice. He gave nothing away. They served two tours together, but he hadn't seen Fox since he was shot in the leg and came home. Mason's incident had happened a few years before Reade's twenty.

"Needed some air. The cabin's too hot. She doesn't like the A/C." It wasn't a complete lie, but one that should appease Fox.

"Got it. I told Carter to get some sleep, so it's just me for a few hours. I'm going to make another pass around the perimeter then take my place out front. You good with that?"

"Yeah. No one's coming in from the lake side. He'd be hiking for miles in order to get in that way."

"Do you think that nut Morris came right up the driveway to deposit those photos in the house?"

"Can't say, but maybe. He got past me, and that pisses me off. I won't let him get close to her again." Which meant he had to find a way to convince her not to go to that major renovation.

"That was a ballsy move. He was watching. He knew when you left with her."

"That wasn't ballsy. He's too much of a coward to stand us down. He really thinks he's in love with her. Misread everything she said on television and social media to mean she was in love with him too. It's a mental illness." He'd done his research on that too. He wasn't an expert, but more than once someone with issues believed a celebrity wanted them because of things they said to the media.

Benjamin Morris needed help, but he had committed several crimes. Reade wanted him off the streets no matter what. He wouldn't allow that guy to hurt Bebe.

"I don't think he wants to face down her body-guards. He took that shot at her from a few hundred feet away. The space was wide open. He was probably on a roof top. He won't have that leverage out here. He'd have to climb into a tree to get a round off, and we would see him." Fox made a gun shape with his fingers and pointed his hand toward the trees.

"What do you think about working on this team?" He could always trust Mason when they were in the field together. He was smart and sure.

"Beats the private investigator work I was doing. This group makes me feel like my skills are still needed. The other way I was busy sitting around watching people cheating on their spouses and having to report that back. That sucked."

"I hear you." But he wasn't sure if he was cut out for this work. Sure, he could do the job itself with his eyes closed, but he'd allowed his emotions to get in the way on this one. He'd never want to leave Bebe's side if she continued to stay in the spotlight.

He wanted to kick something. She wasn't his to take care of. She was the client. And he didn't plan on sticking around. He had figured Lincoln could send him on assignments anywhere; that was why he had agreed to come on board in the first place.

"Get some sleep," Fox said. "You look like shit." He returned the way he came.

"Thanks, dickhead."

"Who are you talking to?" Bebe stood in the doorway. She had slid the door open while he was talking to Mason, and again he'd missed it.

What the fuck was happening to him?

"Mason Fox. He came around back to check on things. What are you doing up?" He pushed out of the chair so he could face her.

She had put on his shirt. The fabric hung to her knees, revealing her bare legs below. She had only secured a few of the buttons, covering the important stuff, but not leaving a whole lot to the imagination. His groin grew hard in his jeans, but he was glad Fox had disappeared already. He had no right to feel possessive of her, but looking that beautiful in his shirt with her hair messed because he caused it gave him some leeway.

"You weren't in bed. I thought maybe I had scared you off."

His attraction—he would never be able to deny—pulled him to her. He gripped her hips and pressed her against him. In seconds, she would feel how he was anything but scared off. "I don't know how to navigate me and you."

"Do we have to figure everything out tonight? I just want to go back inside with you." She gripped his shoulders.

"I don't want you to go to that renovation." He did want to take her back to bed and make her call out his name again. She could even leave on the shirt. But he couldn't keep his mouth shut about her work.

"It's not up to you." She tapped his chest.

"I can't keep you safe. There will be too many variables I can't control. Once the network announces you will be there, that's going to be a green light for Morris to show up."

"They need me."

"Let them use someone else."

"I can't. It's for a woman who has lived in the inner city for years. She has a one-bedroom apartment where she's raising her two kids and her sister's three. She has to duck bullets on her way to work every morning. She worries one of the kids will get shot trying to get to school. I've been asked to renovate the house and decorate it for her so she can give her family a better life. I'm going." She pushed away from him, almost knocking him off-balance.

"The man broke into your house. You saw those pictures. What is it going to take to talk some sense into you?"

"I admit this thing between us happened quickly. I didn't see it coming, and I don't regret what we just did, but you are nothing more than my bodyguard. It's not like we're in love or something. I don't owe you any explanations." She marched inside and slammed the door shut.

He dropped into the chair and hung his head. She was wrong. About part of it. She might not be, but he was. In love. And in trouble.

BEBE SNUCK past Reade fast asleep on the couch. The

lines on his face had softened in slumber. The earlier anger was washed away. His long legs extended past the edge of the couch, and the guilt made her draw a breath. She hadn't meant for him to sleep out here.

He hadn't come back inside until the sun started to color the sky in oranges and yellows. She had peeked from the bedroom window after she went in the house. He had sat in that chair for hours, tapping his fingers on the arm. She regretted what she had said in anger. She had hurt him and never intended for that to happen. And she had lied to protect her heart. He was so much more than her bodyguard, but how could she admit she had strong feelings for a man she hardly knew? People would think she was crazy. And maybe she was.

When he hadn't come back to bed, her heart ached. She had caused her own pain, but she had hoped he would at least lie beside her. She had wanted to curl against his strength and inhale his scent. Even apologize for her hasty words. She had kept his shirt on all night. He had probably given her the space she had demanded with that dramatic exit because that would be Reade. He paid attention to the details.

Now, she needed to burn off some energy. Her ankle felt fine. She would take a walk through the woods with one of the other bodyguards because she still wasn't ready to go back into her cabin and start renovations.

If she couldn't work on her own projects, how was she going to help a woman in desperate need of her skills? Her creativity seemed to have dried up with the gunshot wound.

She couldn't worry about that. By the time she had to arrive on set, she would figure out her problems. She had asked Stuart to send her the photos of the house as is. Something would click.

Which was why she needed the walk. Whenever she had burnout, she returned to nature. Immersing herself among the colors, scents, and textures of the outdoors always helped her find her center again. She eased the front door closed so as not to wake Reade. He deserved some rest. He hadn't really slept in two nights.

"Good morning," a male voice said.

She jumped. "Geez. I didn't see you there." She took a few deep breaths to still her heart.

"Sorry about that. We haven't officially met. I'm Mason Fox." He held out his hand.

She slipped hers into his strong grip. Mason Fox was almost as tall as Reade. Mason was well-built, but not as muscular as Reade. Mason was handsome in a GQ kind of way with his pronounced chin, high cheekbones, and latte-colored skin. Mason's eyes were a startling hazel, and his high-voltage smile lit up his face but didn't quite make it to those winter lake-like eyes.

She wasn't afraid of Mason. He was part of this

team, and this team was the very best. She should know. She'd written the check. Those eyes must have a story, though. One that maybe she could hear eventually, but today she needed space to think.

"It's nice to finally meet you. I'm going for a walk. Reade is still asleep. I didn't want to wake him. Can you or someone else go with me?"

Mason smirked. Did he suspect what happened between her and Reade? Or had Reade said something? Heat ran up her neck and spread across her cheeks. She forced her face to stay neutral and hoped it worked.

"I'm about to take a break. I've been up all night, but Boone will go with you. I'll let him know you're heading out. Do you want to wait for him? He's in the truck." Mason pointed halfway down the drive where the pickup sat under a low hanging branch.

"Will he be long?" She wanted to get started and out of there before Reade realized. He'd insist on going with her. She needed to get her wits about her before they spoke again.

"Not sure, actually. But I will hurry him along."

"I really don't want to wait." She also needed to prove to Reade she was fine by herself in certain circumstances, or he would never relent about her avoiding this new reno.

"Ma'am, I'd rather you wait for Boone. Reade will kick my ass if I let you go alone."

There hadn't been any sightings of Benjamin

Morris since the photos. These men had stood guard all night. Reade seemed certain Morris wouldn't hang around with all the extra protection. "I'll be fine for a few minutes until Boone can catch up. I'll use the path by the lake."

"I have to follow orders. Reade said you can't go out alone. Ever. He's the boss. He's in charge."

"Well, Reade isn't the boss of me. Tell Boone not to waste time. I'm getting started." And with that, she turned her back on Mason Fox.

Who did Reade think he was dictating her every step? She was a grown woman with a mind of her own and had done just fine before Reade came into her life.

She marched down the path and hooked a hard left at the lake. Sure, she had hired a bodyguard because her world had shattered in a million pieces, but she could still take care of herself to some degree. Maybe her father had been right about having a gun. If she had a gun with her now, she wouldn't need Reade at all.

The trees became dense, making it harder for the sun to penetrate their leaves. The ground was covered in sticks and branches. Her feet crunched over dried leaves dropped from autumns past. She kept the lake to her right and glanced over from time to time, making sure it stayed with her.

Reade didn't understand what was at stake for her. These women that she helped were actually helping her. It was her way to give back for having been so fortunate. Stuart hated that she did these renos too, but not for the same reason as Reade. Stuart didn't want to waste resources on projects he couldn't profit from. He didn't give a damn about giving back. But that wasn't Reade. He had sacrificed himself for his country. A man who went to war to keep other people safe was a hero. Her ex-husband was just an asshole.

She glanced again to her right and couldn't see the lake. Her breath picked up speed. She turned in circles. Trees surrounded her from every angle. Somehow, she'd gone off track because she was too busy thinking about Reade.

Her property was fifty acres and butted up to other large natural areas. She had no idea how far away from her cabin she was. She clenched her fists to keep her hands from shaking. A solution existed. Somewhere.

A bird called out in the distance. She jumped. A squirrel scurried past. Her heart pounded behind her ribs. Her phone. She would call Reade. He could tell her how to find her way back. His Army Ranger skills must include navigating terrain. She patted her pants pockets.

Nothing.

CHAPTER 13

"WHERE IS SHE?" Reade fought the urge to grab Boone by the collar and punch his face.

Boone and Mason stared at him.

"I told her to wait," Mason said. "But she was in a hurry. I grabbed Carter, but by the time he jumped out of the truck she was gone."

"I trailed her," Boone said. "She left some prints in the damp soil, but she must've gone into the woods from the point near the lake. I lost her there."

"Did you call out to her?" These guys weren't amateurs. She couldn't have gotten too far, and yet they lost her. While he was asleep.

She had ducked out on him, and that felt like a kick to the gut. He understood why she was pissed about what he said, but to just leave without even telling him, and then to leave her phone behind. That move spoke volumes.

He was being overprotective of her when he had no right. She was supposed to be only the client, but when he took her to bed that changed everything. He may have had encounters with women without ties in the past, but this time it was different. He didn't care how that made him sound. He needed to find her. Now.

"Man, what do you think? I tracked and yelled until my throat went dry. She has to be walking in circles if she doesn't have a compass," Boone said.

"You need to spread out. Make your perimeter wider. Mason, you take the northeast section. Boone, you go southwest and circle back. I'll cut through the middle and double back. We're not going to miss her this time."

"Someone should stay behind to keep an eye on the place," Mason said.

Mason brought up a good point. Reade dug his phone out of his pocket and punched at the screen until a call rang on the other end.

"Montero. Speak." Jax Montero picked up right away.

"Please tell me you're still at the end of the driveway watching the road." He didn't try to hide the growl in his voice.

"Where the hell would I have gone? Is there a problem?"

He told Jax about how Bebe went missing. "I need

you to come up to the cabin and keep watch while we go looking for her."

"I'll call Linc. He can send someone to take my place out at the road so we don't miss anything. Morris hasn't been located so we have to keep eyes wide open. I'm turning the truck around now. I'll be up there in three. This is a royal screw up. Linc's going to want someone's head."

"Like I don't know that." He ended the call. "He's on his way. Head out. I won't be far behind. Your first call is to me when you find her."

Mason and Boone took off in their respective directions. A truck's engine rumbled up the driveway. Jax laid on the horn and gave a wave.

He took off toward the woods. "Where are you, Bebe? Come back to me."

If anything happened to her, he'd never forgive himself. As soon as he saw her, he would apologize. Then quit.

BEBE PASSED the same tree again. If she hadn't found a rock and carved an X in the soft bark, she wouldn't know which tree it was. She was lost. Her feet and legs ached from all the miles she clocked just going in circles. Her stomach growled, reminding her she had never bothered to eat before she left the house because she had been in a rush to get away from

Reade. Well, she regretted that decision now. If she had put her pride aside for five minutes, she would have a bodyguard with her who would know how to lead her out.

She only hoped by now Reade had realized she was missing and sent out the troops for her. Her plan to prove to him she could take care of herself fell on its face. He would never leave her side for a second now, and he would fight her every inch not to do that reno. That left her with two choices—agree to what he asked or fire him. She didn't want to do either.

Something snapped behind her like a small branch breaking. She stopped and looked over her shoulder. "Reade?" The trees behind her stood inches apart, making it difficult to tell if anyone or anything was back there. Some of the trunks were thick while others were thinner. Many were covered in moss, but she couldn't find any sign of Reade or the other bodyguards.

"Reade?" She tried again.

No response. The sound of a snapping twig must've been a pine cone falling or a rabbit running. She continued forward, hoping she hadn't traveled this way yet. The snap came again. A chill ran down her back. A rabbit wouldn't make that sound.

"Who's there?" She spun around, but she couldn't find anything except the trees and their swaying branches.

Her heart picked up pace. She was being ridiculous

and took a few deep calming breaths. She wasn't sure which way she wanted to go now. Her sudden movement threw her off. She couldn't even find the tree with the X carved in it. Whichever way she decided, she did not want to go in the direction of that last snap, especially if it were an animal larger than a rabbit.

She hurried along, trying to ignore the tightness in her chest. Dried leaves crunched and crackled behind her. She stole a quick glance. Something red dashed between some of the trees.

She ran. Her legs pumped, forcing her forward. Her lungs struggled to keep up. She didn't dare risk a look behind her again. Looking back would slow her down. Whatever might be following her or not, she needed to put space between her and it just the same.

She leaped over a downed tree and caught the toe of her shoe on the trunk. She sprawled on her hands and face. The wet ground squished between her fingers. Leaves flew in her mouth. Her hair covered her face, making it impossible to see. She paused for a second and assessed her ankle. It seemed okay. The breaking of branches and crunching of dried leaves continued behind her.

She forced herself on unsteady legs and ran again. She wanted to find a place to hide. If she closed her eyes to make it all go away like when she was a kid, she would hand herself a death sentence. Whether an animal or human was behind her, she wouldn't stand a chance. She pushed on and hoped her legs wouldn't give out.

She banged into brush. The branches and thorns scraped at her arms and legs and drew blood. Stopping to check the damage would be the end of her. She had to find the tree line or the lake or even the road. Reade had said someone was stationed by her driveway entrance. Could she get there?

"Bebe." The sound of her name in the wind forced her head around.

She stole a glance while she ran, but no one was behind her. The sensation of someone gaining speed pressed against her as if they were actually reaching out with bony fingers to grab her and yank her back. She might not be able to see anything behind her, but she wasn't alone anymore, and it wasn't Reade or one of the men on his team.

Benjamin Morris was back.

She ran harder. Her lungs burned with each step. A stitch bit her side. She stumbled and grabbed her hip. Footsteps pounding the ground echoed off the trees. Branches broke and leaves split from something trampling them. Or someone. Someone who knew her name.

The sunlight grew brighter in the distance as if breaking the woods apart. Relief gave her the strength to carry on. But with every step the end seemed farther away. The side of her cabin peeked through the sun's rays. She might actually make it to the clearing ahead.

The distance to safety closed up. She kept her gaze on the red clapboards of her cabin, praying what she saw wasn't her imagination.

One of the bodyguards had to be waiting there, didn't they? She fought the urge to take a final look behind at whatever could be chasing her before she opened her mouth to yell for help.

And collided with a solid mass.

CHAPTER 14

BEBE SCREAMED. Her fists struck hard while she kept her eyes closed. She would fight. It's what Reade would want her to do.

"Bebe, it's me."

She continued to scream and flail, making contact but not making headway.

"Sweetheart, it's me. Look at me. You're okay. I'm here." Reade gripped her wrists and pulled her against him.

She gulped in air and stared up him. His tender eyes stared back. She wanted to run her fingers over his bearded face. He had found her. Relief made her knees weak. She slumped against him, then looked over her shoulder again. "Someone's chasing me. He called my name." She pointed into the woods.

He helped her into the clearing. The sun hurt her eyes, but the wide-open space made her lungs expand for the first time in hours. She gripped his arm slung over her shoulders, keeping her close. If she let go of him, she would drown.

"Mason, take her." Reade pushed her toward Mason and ran.

"Wait. You can't go in there." Reade disappeared into the woods. "Where's he going?" She tried to run after him, but Mason pulled her back.

"Let's get you inside."

She struggled against his hold, but Mason was strong. With one hand, he held her in place and opened the front door to Reade's cabin. He put her on the couch and locked the door. She jumped back up, but he stood like a sentry. He holstered a large gun, but the glare in his eyes said he meant business. Even with her.

"You have to help him. Benjamin Morris is in the woods." She couldn't sit. She paced the small space between the window and the kitchen area.

"You need to stay put. Reade is the most skilled guy on our team. Boone and Jax are out there with him so he has plenty of excellent backup. Lincoln is at the road. No one fucks with Linc. Those men won't let Morris get away."

"I can't stay here."

"You have to for now. Reade's number one priority is keeping you safe. I'm not going against that order. You're bleeding. Why don't you clean up those scratches?" He didn't budge from his place by the door.

This man wasn't going to allow a little blood to soften him, not if he was an Army Ranger like Reade. Mason had seen his fair share of blood she guessed. His eyes were vacant of any tender emotion, and his jaw was set. She headed for the bathroom.

"And don't think about climbing out the window, either. I can run a hundred meters in thirteen seconds."

She assumed that was fast, but she didn't want to go after Reade. She wanted him to come back safe and sound. Then she wanted to pack her bags and find another place to live that Benjamin Morris would never find.

He was here. He had been in the woods following her. It had to be him. Who else could it have been? Could one of the men on Reade's team have called out her name? They must've been searching for her. She'd been gone for hours and wasn't supposed to be left alone.

Logic told her the voice in the wind had come from Morris. He had broken into her home and touched her things. An icy dread ran over her skin. He had watched her with an eagle eye, taking pictures of her. She was grateful he'd never seen her nude, but would she be safe?

Her hands shook as she opened the cabinet door

under the sink. The only thing under there was another roll of toilet paper. She hadn't asked for rubbing alcohol or hydrogen peroxide to be brought before her arrival. She closed her eyes and blew out a long breath. The morning scare pushed her to the floor. She pulled her knees to her chest. What a stupid thing not to ask for. She had wanted both cabins stocked for their comfort, but she'd forgotten a simple thing like bandages. A hysterical laugh escaped her lips. She smacked her hand over her mouth to keep the rest in. Like a lightning bolt, the next thought burned through her. She ran back out to the living area.

"Mason, is it possible someone from the realtor's office told Benjamin Morris about me buying this property?"

"Anything's possible. Did you use your name?"

"I didn't. I bought it in my mother's name, but I had been spotted in town before I moved in. I was at that cute little general store. The owner...I can't remember her name...she was sweet. She said she watched the show. I tried to act like she had the wrong person, but she winked at me. It was harmless. I even forgot about it until two seconds ago. Could she have mentioned seeing me?"

"We'll tell Reade and the others when they return. It's a lead they can follow. You're still bleeding." He gave a nod in her direction.

Sure enough blood trickled down her leg and into her sock. "Can you get me some bandages?"

"No can do. Sorry. My orders are to stay right here with you until Reade comes back. Apply pressure with a towel. If you need stitches, I'm pretty good with a needle."

"Do you happen to have a needle?" She raised her brow in question. This man and his orders infuriated her.

He pulled out a utility knife from a pocket on his pants.

She shook her head. "No, thanks." She went back into the bathroom to clean up the dirt from her legs and hands.

Reade still hadn't returned. She wasn't sure if she could wait much longer. She wanted to be anywhere but Winter, Montana.

But with Mason standing guard, making a break for it could prove to be a big mistake.

READE HUNG HIS HEAD. The whole day had been a bust. They couldn't find any trace of Benjamin Morris. For all he knew, Bebe had allowed her imagination to run away with itself while she was lost. Considering what she had been through, it wasn't a far stretch to think she had overreacted. The mind played tricks. He knew that too well. His mind was even trying to convince him he was in love with her.

The taillights of Jax's and Linc's pickups dwindled

into the darkness. The sun had set while Linc blew a gasket over what had happened. He was lucky to still have a job, but he couldn't be impartial any longer. That was a problem, though he hadn't admitted it to his boss. He would talk to Bebe first, but then he would have to resign from this assignment. Linc had other men he could put on Bebe.

Boone lit a cigarette. The smell of sulfur drifted toward him. "Want one?" Boone said.

"No, thanks."

"This wasn't your fault." He took a drag. The end of the cigarette glowed red.

"Sure it is. She went off without protection, and Benjamin Morris could be within yards of us right now and no one would know it. I missed it all. Doesn't make me much of a bodyguard."

"It's been a long day. Call it a night. Fox is getting some sleep. I'll keep watch here. Linc's got the driveway covered. Your lady needs you."

"She's not my lady."

"Yeah, okay. Keep telling yourself that." Boone took another drag and stamped his cigarette out on the bottom of his boot. He pocketed what was left of the butt and took up his place at the foot of the walkway.

Reade couldn't stall any longer. He had to face Bebe, and opened the door with a heavy sigh. She was curled up on the couch fast asleep. He stole a minute to take her in. The blanket covered the curves he had quickly learned to enjoy. Her hair fell in wisps against her face. He resisted the urge to brush it back. She wasn't his. Like he told Boone.

When he had returned empty-handed from hunting down Morris, she had run outside to him, but he stopped her with just a glare. His ego had stung when he woke this morning and she was gone without even leaving a note behind. She had told Linc her story instead of him. He had a lot of apologizing to do.

He squatted down beside her. "Bebe?" His fingers still itched to touch her, but he clenched his fists instead.

She blinked open her eyes. "Hey."

"I'm sorry to wake you. Can we talk a few minutes?" He stood to give her some space.

She pushed up and wiped a hand over her face. The blanket fell from her shoulders. Her white t-shirt showed off her muscular arms and black bra. His mouth watered.

"Any news?"

"There's no sign of him. We've checked every inch of your property. If he was here, he's gone now." He scratched the back of his neck. "I have to ask you this. Are you sure you heard someone call your name?"

"Do you think I made that up?"

"It's just when people are scared, they don't always get the details straight." He wasn't accusing her of anything, but she had been lost, probably tired, and definitely frightened based on her reaction when she had bumped into him.

"I heard him, Reade. Well, I heard someone." She looked at her hands.

He dropped onto the other end of the couch and took up too much space near her. His back burned from all the hiking. Nothing was going to get rid of that pain except maybe her hands on him. Standing wasn't an option any longer, and the kitchen chair would only make things worse.

"Okay, you heard something. But we couldn't find any sign of him." He was too tired to hide his frustration.

"So you've said. And Lincoln said it. And that other guy." She snapped her fingers. "Jax."

"Why didn't you wake me?" He had to know what she had been thinking. "If Morris had been in those woods this morning, who knows what could have happened to you." His trembling voice betrayed him.

She put a hand on his thigh. The heat from her touch went straight to his core. He wanted her hands all over him, and that was part of the problem. He should be grilling her for details, and all he wanted to do was make love to her. He wanted to erase the dark circles under her eyes and the lines around her mouth that had deepened.

"I was so mad at you for last night, and I felt badly for you at the same time. I know you stayed up most of the night because of me. I wanted you to get some sleep, and I wanted some space to figure out what's happening between us."

"You can't go out alone. Do you hear me?" What would he do if something happened to her? He would never forgive himself if she were hurt.

"Reade, I made a mistake. I won't do that again, but I can't stay here. I need to find another place to live."

"Does that mean you won't do the show?"

"It doesn't mean that. That woman's future is in my hands. I can't let her down."

"Give the responsibility to someone else." He pushed away from her, ignoring the pain running down his legs. He didn't know how to make her understand he would fall apart if something happened to her.

She jumped off the couch and stood inches from him. She tilted up her pretty chin. He wanted to cup her face and kiss the hell out of her. That feisty side made his dick hard.

"What kind of person will I be if I walk away from my responsibilities? Would you leave someone behind who was hurt and needing you?"

"It's the not the same thing."

"Looks the same to me. You would never leave behind a man on your team."

"This woman isn't on any team with you."

"She's a woman trying to take care of her family. She wants a good life for her children. She wants to feel safe at night. That is exactly my team, and I have the power to make it happen for her. I know you have strong feelings for me, because I have them for you too. Some people will think we're out of minds when we tell them our story, but if you're going to fall for me, you have to fall for all of me. No halfway relationships. I've already done that. I won't do it again."

He gripped her hips and pulled her against him. "Our story, huh?"

She ducked her head and her hair covered her face. He brushed it away so he could see the light in her eyes when she brought her gaze to his.

"Don't try to distract me from the point." She smiled for him.

"I believe the point you're making is I have to accept all of you. Even the stuff I might not like."

"Just like I have to accept all of you. And that includes you having a dangerous job because I wouldn't ask you to give it up if this is what you want to do."

"I don't know if I want to stay." There, he had said it.

"Why not?" She wrapped her arms around his neck and ran her fingers over his skin.

"I won't be able to think straight if you continue to do that."

"Try." Her eyes sparkled with a devilish hue. She continued to drive him crazy with her soft touch.

Oh yeah, he was in big trouble with this lady.

"I don't want to talk about my job right now." He kissed her neck below her ear. Her sweet smell intoxicated him. He held her bottom with both hands to keep her pressed against him.

She moaned and leaned into him as his lips traveled down her neck. His jeans grew more uncomfortable each time she rubbed against him.

"I just want to say that while you were gone all day, the only thing I wanted was to see you come through the tree line unhurt. I didn't care about anything else. That's when I knew."

"Knew what?" he said with his lips still on her neck. She tasted like the outdoors. He wanted to run his tongue over every part of her, especially the places that would make her call out his name and tremble from his touch.

"Knew I wouldn't be able to live without you."

He tore his lips away to meet her stare. "Don't say something you don't mean."

"I mean it with every fiber of my being. I don't care how crazy I sound. I've never been so attracted or connected to another person as quickly as you. It was as if from the first moment I saw you, I knew you and I were meant to be together."

He had never believed in destiny or fate or any of that bullshit. He believed in hard work, following orders, and keeping his head on straight. Until this woman walked into his life and flipped all that upside down.

"Then you know if we're together, I have to keep you safe. That will always be the thing that matters most to me. I don't care how possessive that sounds. My woman will never worry with me around."

"I'm not backing down on that reno, Reade. Deal with it. And if you can't, get your hands off my ass."

He barked out a laugh. "You are a tough lady."

"I had to be. Can you live with my condition?"

"I can't live without you." He swooped her up in his arms and carried her to the bedroom.

"Then that's a yes." She smiled up at him.

"Let me show you how much of a yes that is."

And he stripped off all her clothes.

CHAPTER 15

READE'S PHONE vibrated against the end table, waking him from the best sleep he'd had in days. He peeled himself from Bebe's warm body with regret, but he had to shut up that phone.

An email had come in. He shook the fog from his brain and opened the app. His blood ran cold. He was fully awake now.

Mr. Brewer,

I saw you touching Bebe tonight. She belongs to me. She loves me and I love her. You had no right. I'm coming for you. And then I'm going to punish her for betraying me by showing everyone what I saw.

Morris had written more, but the attachment of photos made Reade's vision blur with anger. He would find this man and strangle the life out of him. He jumped to the window. Nothing unusual appeared in the dark. The curtains were see-through, though. Had Morris been watching from the other side while he and Bebe made love? His stomach turned. He couldn't tell her. It would devastate her.

His phone vibrated in his hand this time. He was ready to give Morris something to be frightened of, but the call was from Lincoln.

"Brewer." His voice came out still pocked with sleep.

"Sorry to bother you at this hour, but I've got information," Lincoln said.

"Hang on." He grabbed his jeans off the floor and shoved in his legs. With bare feet, and the zipper undone, he padded outside. He wanted to hear what Linc had to say, but he didn't want Bebe to accidentally overhear him in that small cabin.

"Okay, what did you find?" He dropped into the chair on the porch.

Mason leaned against the truck and gave a wave. For a second he felt bad one of those men had to stand watch through the night and the other rested in a truck down the drive while he slept in a bed next to a beautiful naked woman who wanted him. But that feeling only lasted for a second.

"I checked into Bebe's idea that someone might've spilled about her being in town. Unfortunately, it looks like Molly Atkins, the owner of the Winter General Store, told her book club that Bebe had been in purchasing items for her new house. Molly was a little starstruck. Winter doesn't see celebrities. She might've spilled which house it was."

"Then one of those women told someone else?"

"Maybe. Molly holds the meetings in the store. She thinks she remembers a man browsing that night."

He stifled a groan. In a town this size, a stranger would stick out, especially around observant women. "Did you show her a photo of Morris?"

"I did. She's pretty sure it was him. Said he kept to himself but kind of lurked near the back where they meet. He gave a few of the ladies the creeps."

"That explains how he knew where her house was." He clenched his fists to keep from punching something. "He reached out to me."

"What do you mean? Are you talking about Morris?"

He told Lincoln about the email. "I don't know if I should tell Bebe."

"She has a right to know. More importantly, send me the email. I want to see if we can't trace the IP address."

"It's coming right now." He tapped the screen and hit the send button.

Bebe probably did have a right to know about Morris's correspondence, but he didn't want to scare her. He also didn't want her worrying about him. "Now what?"

"Hank is canvassing the area to see if Morris has

shown up anywhere else like a hotel, local retailers, wherever. Morris probably wanted to talk to others to gain information about Bebe."

"How did he track her once she arrived in Montana?"

"We haven't figured that out yet. But that's a moot point now. He's here."

He had hoped Bebe had been wrong about hearing someone call her name in the woods. Based on the time they could pinpoint it down to, he and the other guys weren't in that area. No one had called out for her that was on his team. He doubted she fabricated the part about someone chasing her either. But if she had? That would explain how she stayed ahead of anyone on her heels. Unless, Morris wanted her to think she was safe for now.

"Reade, are you listening?"

"Yeah." No. He stole a quick glance at the door to make sure Bebe wasn't eavesdropping.

"Unless Morris does something else, there isn't a lot we can do to him. We don't know where he is. The partial print we found in Bebe's house isn't enough of a match to get him on breaking and entering. We want to get him for something bigger, though. If he's arrested for stalking, the most he would see is five years behind bars in this state. I know you don't want to hear this, but if he puts his hands on her, we could get him for something that would keep him away for a lot longer."

"You want to use her as bait?" His body trembled. She could get hurt or worse. He had said he agreed to that damn show, but listening to Linc only made what needed to be done too real. She wasn't trained for something like this. She'd be a sitting duck.

"She's got that reno show coming up. The network is allowing fans to watch the build from behind the wood barricades. He might show up there, thinking he'll have another chance," Linc said.

"I can't allow her to get shot again." A pain built behind his eyes. He pressed his fingers into his lids, but the pain didn't subside.

"She can't hide forever. Guys like Morris won't go away. He believes she's in love with him. The email said as much."

"She could get seriously hurt." He stated the obvious, but the words still scraped his throat raw. He couldn't lose her.

"I know you're trying to protect her, and this was supposed to be an easy job, but things changed. If she's out in public, we have a chance of catching him."

Lincoln had a point and so had Bebe. It didn't mean he had to like it.

"I want to go over every possible scenario until I'm certain she has it. No mistakes on this."

"No one can guarantee a mission without mistakes, you know that. But I promise you, we'll do everything in our power to keep her safe. You have my word." He ended the call.

What if Linc's word wasn't enough? Reade scrolled back to his emails. Bile burned his throat as he reread Morris's words. He would put his hands around this guy's neck and choke the life out of him if Morris laid one finger on Bebe.

"Reade?" Bebe stood in the doorway, wearing his shirt again. The light behind her cast her body in a dark shadow.

He fumbled his phone, dropping it on the ground. She reached for it, but he swiped it away. "When did you come out here?"

She narrowed her eyes. "I woke up, and you were gone. The door wasn't completely closed. I heard your voice. Is something wrong?"

"No." He shoved his phone into his back pocket and considered zipping his pants so she'd take him seriously.

"Then who were you talking to at this hour?"

"Lincoln." He decided to zip his pants after all. If he was going to keep things from her, he should at least be dressed.

"Did something happen?"

"Nothing good. He agrees with you about the show. You'll be happy to know."

"Good. Now come back to bed." She put her hand out.

He kept his gaze on her hand. She didn't have to

know that Morris had found them out. He didn't want her ending things because of what had happened between them, but he didn't want to lie to her either.

"Reade? What is going on?" She clenched the collar of the shirt in her fist.

He cleared the space between them and pulled her into his arms. She relaxed against him. The warmth of her body against his bare chest sent all his heat to his groin. This was the only place he wanted to be. He wouldn't consider pulling up roots after being with her like this. She stared up at him with wide eyes. He had a decision to make.

"Morris sent me an email."

"What?" She pushed out of his arms, but he held her close.

"It's okay."

"That's why you didn't want me to see your phone. What did he say?"

He fished his phone out of his pocket and opened the email for her to read. Her face went pale as her gaze scanned the screen.

"He saw us? Where is he? Is he here?" The look in her eyes went wild. She bolted for the house, and he ran after her.

She pulled all the curtains closer together and ran around the small space, turning off any light that had remained on and threw them into darkness.

"I think I'm going to be sick," she said. "How did he see us?"

"Probably some kind of a lens." He followed her heavy breathing until he reached her standing by the edge of the sofa. He gathered her in his arms again. She shivered in his embrace.

"Will he put those pictures on the internet?" Tears leaked from her eyes and wet his chest.

"We don't even know if he has any pictures, but he does seem to know you and I are a thing." He needed to believe Morris was trying to get the best of him and didn't have any photos. Morris couldn't have come close enough to the house to get any pictures of them in bed. Mason and Boone would've heard him. The trees would've been an interference from the distance of the woods. Taking photos would explain why he had been in the woods in the first place.

"Reade, everyone will see them. My father. My God." She sobbed.

He stroked her back, hoping to calm her down. Balancing a woman's emotions had never been something he was good at. "We'll get him before he has a chance to do anything."

Morris promised to expose those pictures of Bebe to her fans for being unfaithful to him, if she didn't make a public apology. Reade bit back the desire to laugh at how ridiculous Morris sounded, but if he had pictures of Bebe in a compromising position, it would destroy her. He didn't give a damn about himself, but he didn't want her to be humiliated because Morris was sick in the head.

"We need to get out on social media and promote the show," she said with conviction.

"He'll take that as your message to him." He wanted to see her face, but he didn't risk turning the light on yet. She was one smart lady coming up with that idea and knowing what it would mean, and that made him want her all over again.

"At least we can try and control when he'll attack me and maybe keep those pictures from turning up anywhere."

"He isn't going to get near you because I'm not letting you out of my sight until this is over and we can finally start a real life together."

"I'm not naive. He might say he's in love with me, but that translates to something evil. He's going to wait for the minute you aren't looking to come for me, and there might not be anything you or I can do about it."

"What are you saying?"

"I'm saying if we play this wrong, you and I won't have any kind of life together. I'll be dead."

CHAPTER 16

Bebe's stomach twisted in knots. They were getting ready to film the big reveal. She, Stuart, and the crew had worked around the clock to make this house spectacular. Surprisingly, she and Stuart managed to get along off camera. It might have had something to do with the fact Reade was never more than six feet away from her and kept a perpetual glare on his face. No one was allowed around her without his permission. She had to admit, part of her liked it.

"Are you okay?" Reade placed a hand on her lower back. His presence gave her the extra courage she needed to get through whatever happened today.

"I think so." As much as she wanted Morris caught, the idea he could fire bullets into the crowd or at her made her heart stutter.

A crowd the size of thousands gathered behind those flimsy barricades. Because they were outside and the reveal required them to move around the property, Reade couldn't be as close as he was when they filmed the stages of the reno. She gripped her middle, hoping the knots in her stomach would unwind or her heart would slow down. No such luck.

"We've got guys in the crowd on the lookout for Morris. Hank stationed men on the roof of houses across the street. See the man behind the camera?"

"The one with the red baseball hat?" She had seen him earlier during the sound check, but she didn't know him.

"He's one of ours too. I'll be right out of the shot over there." He pointed to a spot about thirty feet away near the barricade. "I'm not going to let anything happen to you." He leaned in and whispered in her ear.

His warm breath sent shivers over her skin. She would rather be safe at home with him than here exposed, but she had a promise to keep. After this show, she would take a year off and recharge the way she had wanted to when she came to Montana. She could still renovate houses, just not on television.

She turned to Reade and placed a hand on his bearded cheek. "I never would've guessed when I arrived in this state, I would find you."

He gripped her hand. "When I took this job, I thought I was going to hate babysitting a high-maintenance celebrity. I never expected to fall for her."

"I'm glad you like surprises."

He pressed a soft kiss on her lips. "Remember what we went over?"

"Duck if I hear gunshots. Get behind anything that could provide cover. Don't be a hero."

"Right. That's my job. He might not even be here. This whole day could go off without a hitch. We haven't heard from him all week. We might have caught a lucky break if he decided he wasn't interested in you any longer."

"I can only hope, but I think my luck has run out. He was in those woods, and he was in my house."

Lincoln jogged over to them. His long hair bounced on his shoulders. "We're all set. All my men are in place. If this goes as planned, by tonight, Benjamin Morris will be behind bars. Bebe, one more time, what are you going to say when you address the crowd during the first scene break?"

This was the part that had her stomach screwy. Lincoln had made the network announce she and Stuart were through and had been. The news led on many outlets so she could make her big announcement today and draw Morris out. She had to correctly say the phrase Reade planned to make Morris angry. "I'm marrying the one and only love of my life. Reade and I are engaged."

"Places everyone." The stage manager waved her hands in the air.

She took a deep breath. Show time.

THE CROWD ROARED. Their energy vibrated as they clapped and cheered at Bebe's announcement. She stood on the front lawn of her latest renovation and showed off the fake diamond ring purchased for this operation. Even Stuart believed her proclamation, if his jaw on the ground was any indication. Reade straightened his shoulders. *That's right, pal. She's mine.* The engagement might be fake, but the feelings were real.

He held his position at the side of the house near the crowd. All of these people wanted a piece of Bebe and Stuart as if they had a right to be in their lives. And in many ways, they did. He would never like this life. Never.

Still no sign of Morris. His earpiece crackled as each man on the team checked-in. Morris wasn't there. This whole charade was a bust. Or maybe Morris had moved on.

"Five minutes, people," the director said.

He stole the opportunity to speak with Bebe. Her makeup person dusted her face with some fan-looking brush. He placed a hand on her elbow. She jumped.

"It's just me."

Her smile spread in a slow easy line. "Hey."

The makeup person with curly hair and a body the width of a two-by-four smirked and rolled her eyes. "Gross. Lovebirds." She closed up her bag and walked away.

"Did I interrupt?" Not that he cared if he had. He wanted her to know he was right there.

"Nah. I'm sweating off that makeup in seconds anyway. I expected there to be a shootout after I announced we were engaged. Do you think this means he isn't here?"

"Most likely." He and his team had planned on Morris using this venue as a way to get attention. No other time would give him the spotlight like this one. If Morris wasn't on this set, then he wasn't coming.

"Now what?" she said.

"You finish filming your show. We go home." And he could focus on making plans to stay in town with Bebe. He allowed his shoulders to drop for the first time in weeks.

"But what if he comes back?"

"We'll be ready." Because he wasn't leaving her. He'd quit working for Linc to protect Bebe full time. He could live off his pension for now. And when Morris was either caught or enough time had gone by that he wasn't a threat anymore, he could go back to construction.

"Hey, Bebe, could you come back here a second?" Stuart waved from the front door of the house.

"What's up? We're about to start and the final reveal sign isn't here."

"I think you need to see this. Now. Hey, Doug, we

need ten," Stuart said to the director. He wanted to smack Stuart upside his big head for bossing Bebe around all the time.

"I don't want to miss the lighting. Hurry up." Doug threw his hands in the air.

"Bebe, please." Stuart went inside as if Bebe would follow without question.

"I'm sorry, Reade. I need to see what's going on. There must be a pipe soldered incorrectly, or he's not sure how the lighting will reflect off his spray tan." She rolled her eyes.

"I'll go with you." He was probably being overprotective. His team had every angle of this event covered. Morris couldn't be within a mile of this place.

"I'll only be a minute. I've walked through the house a hundred times today. Nothing is wrong in there except Stuart's ego. But if I don't go see whatever it is, he'll never shut up and we'll lose the whole day." She placed a lingering kiss on his lips. She tasted sweet and minty.

"I know a thing or two about construction. I could help."

"I've got this one. Enjoy the sunshine." She started walking away. "I just had an idea." She turned back toward him.

"What's that?"

"When this is all over, how would you feel about going into business with me? No television. Just you and me fixing up houses for people like Roxanne who need a new start."

"I could be persuaded." As long as her ex-husband wasn't in the picture.

"I know lots of ways to persuade you." She blew him a kiss and went into the house, closing the door behind her.

He shoved his hands in his pockets and rocked on his heels. A warmth spread over him at the thought of her persuading him. But there was one very big problem that had to be answered before he and Bebe could have a life together.

Where the hell was Benjamin Morris?

CHAPTER 17

BEBE STARED at the hole in the bottom corner kitchen cabinet then back at Stuart. "How did this happen?"

"The door was left open just enough to let a varmint in." He pointed to the slider between the cabinets and the table.

"What do you think it was? A raccoon or a squirrel?" She squatted down. The wood had been chewed through, leaving a hole the size of a grapefruit.

"Beats me. But I can't find it. Either it went back out or it's in the house someplace. We need to check every room before we let the cameras in here."

"We can't patch this. It's going to mean we have to rip out all of these cabinets and replace them because it's one piece."

"Oh, hell no. If we take out the bottom section of cabinets, then we have to remove the counter, and we'll destroy the backsplash. I will cut out the side panel and put in a new one. She won't even realize. Tell Doug I need thirty minutes. Don't let anyone in here."

"You are not short-changing this woman. We need to bring Roxanne straight into the kitchen right after her initial reaction to the inside. We can continue to film and keep the cameras away from this angle."

"It's the damn side panel. I could put a piece right over it and she'd never know."

"We will do the fix the right way and not cut corners because you don't like difficult jobs."

"Give me a break. This place is a mansion compared to the dump she was living in before. Do you really think it matters if I replace the panel?"

"I want this job done the right way. It's our reputation."

"It's your reputation. You're the do-gooder. I'm just a guy who's good with his hands. If you won't go tell Doug, I will. Go look for that animal that chewed the cabinet so it doesn't jump on me while I'm working." Stuart stormed off before she could say another word.

She seethed inside. For the life of her, she couldn't remember what she had ever seen in that man. She also couldn't believe how well he hid his lack of empathy from the camera. He had everyone fooled.

She pushed open the slider and stood out on the

new patio they poured for Roxanne. The breeze that rolled in did nothing to cool the anger in her veins. She had added a beautiful wood table for Roxanne and her children to sit at and have dinners out here. She ran her fingers over the blue plates she had set to make the table look like it came right out of a magazine. She hadn't left a detail undone. She would never cut a corner in her jobs.

She didn't care one little bit if that rodent jumped on Stuart while he worked. In fact, she hoped it did. She would pay to replace the cabinets herself. Stuart could go screw himself, and she would tell him that now. They would shoot the program the way she wanted and show Roxanne the hole. It was the right thing to do. She reached for the slider.

"Finally, we can be alone, darling. Because you need to explain what it is you think you're doing with that Reade Brewer. You're mine, Bebe. Mine."

She turned as if in slow motion. Ice water pooled in her belly. Her knees buckled under the enormous weight of fear. Benjamin Morris stood on the other side of the patio. A greasy smile slicked his face, his black eyes void of emotion, and he pointed a gun at her.

Her mouth refused to work. She didn't dare blink, but her mind raced to find a solution. Where was Reade? How long would it be before he realized she hadn't returned and would come looking for her?

"What do you want?" Her tongue stuck to the roof of her dry mouth.

"What I've always wanted, the two of us together forever. I know you love me and not Reade. I know he forced himself on you. I saw everything. It wasn't your fault. We can have him arrested for raping you. But you need to come with me now." Sweat beaded on his high forehead. His tongue shot out and licked his lips.

"Please put the gun down." Bile rose up in the back of her throat. She needed to think, but all her thoughts tumbled into each other.

"The gun is for your own good, darling. I know you wanted to save yourself for me, but you were very bad to bring another man into your house without my permission. I can't let you deflower yourself like that again."

"Are you going to shoot me?" She shuffled a half-inch toward the door.

"Only if you're bad again. I didn't mean to shoot you the first time. I'm very sorry about that. I meant to rid us of Stuart. Come on now. We have to go." He rocked back and forth. His free hand twitched at his side.

He was becoming more off-balance. She didn't know what to say. People on television always reasoned with their captor, but her insides shook, making it difficult to breathe. She wasn't sure she could even speak coherently.

"If you loved me, you wouldn't hurt me." Where was Reade? She edged back another half-inch.

"Stop moving." The gun shook in Morris's hand. "Please, darling, we need to leave now."

"I can't leave. I have to finish my show."

"I don't blame you for moving to Montana and making me follow you," he said as if she hadn't spoken. "I blame you for fucking another man. There's a bullet in this gun for Reade, then you and I can go anywhere you want and be together forever. Would you like that?"

She could only stare at him.

"I said, would you like that?" He screamed and his hand shook more. He pounded his leg with his fist.

"Please, don't shoot. Put that gun down. I'll do whatever you ask." Where the hell was Reade? Should she scream for him to come?

"That's better. Now come here." He waved her over with one hand and kept the gun pointed at her with the other.

She took a tentative step forward. He lunged for her and grabbed her by the neck, twisting her around so her back pressed against his chest. He gripped her in place with one arm, his hold as strong as a vise. She struggled against him, but he shoved the gun against her temple.

"Stop that." His free hand ran over her belly and stopped just shy of her crotch.

Sweat slicked her skin. Her stomach burned,

making her sick. She stilled against him and squeezed her eyes shut.

"Let her go." Menace filled Reade's deep voice.

Relief washed over her. He filled up the doorway, holding a big black gun in both hands. He stood strong and sure. His jaw was set, and a death glare filled his eyes. She had never seen him like this. Like a man who wasn't afraid to pull that trigger.

In the kitchen, behind Reade, was Stuart and someone with a camera.

"Can't do that. I love her, and she loves me," Morris said.

"She loves me, you sick son of a bitch. Either let her go, or I'll shoot you between the eyes. Bebe, I've got this. Just keep looking at me." Reade didn't flinch. The gun never wavered.

"If you shoot me, I'll shoot her, so you'll never do it. You're a man trained to follow the rules." Morris tightened his grip on her. She struggled against him.

"You're surrounded, Mr. Morris. Let her go," Lincoln said.

She dared a glance. Lincoln and the other Brotherhood men had come up from the woods without a sound. "Reade?" Her voice wobbled.

"Sweetheart, remember what we talked about in rehearsal?"

She could only nod.

"Morris, this is your last chance. Let her go, or I will kill you." Reade continued to stand steady.

"You won't do any such—"

"Now," Reade shouted.

She ducked. Reade fired. Morris went down. Blood ran over the patio. She collapsed.

CHAPTER 18

BEBE SAT on the front step of the renovated house that was now a crime scene. Her hands shook. Even though the afternoon sun cooked the dirt until it cracked, she was frozen on the inside. She could still feel the pressure of Benjamin Morris's hand on her stomach and the weight of his body pulling hers back as he fell to the ground.

Roxanne and her family were sent to a hotel until her house was cleaned up. Stuart disappeared with his camera guy the second Morris hit the ground. Mason Fox had followed them to retrieve the footage and destroy it.

"Here." Reade handed her a cup of tea. "This will warm you up. And I'm sorry."

"For what?"

The street had been cleared of all the onlookers and fans that had come out for the big reveal. Instead, men in pickup trucks, the team of former military now part of the Brotherhood Protectors, lined the road along with a police car and an ambulance.

"For dropping my guard and allowing that bastard to get his hands on you." He wiped his hands over his face.

"This wasn't your fault. You were amazing." She shielded her eyes from the sun as she looked up at Reade.

"I made too many mistakes because I let my feelings get in the way. You could've been hurt..." He stared off.

"But I wasn't hurt because of you. You saved me." She would be eternally grateful for his quick thinking and stone-cold bravery.

"When you hadn't returned, I felt the chill up the back of my neck. I knew then that I let you down."

"Please come sit with me." He took the spot beside her on the step and held her hand in his. "You did not let me down. Not once. Please believe that."

"I'll try."

"But I have to ask you, how did you really know you would hit him?"

His beard twitched over his smile. "Sweetheart, surrender is not an Army Ranger word."

"But how did you know?"

"Because he led a sniper team for many years," Lincoln said. "You're in good hands with him, Bebe. We're just about finished up here. You can fill out the report tomorrow if you want to take Bebe home. Thank you, Brewer. I'm going to hate to lose you." Lincoln stuck out his hand.

"Wait? You're quitting?"

"I told Linc before all this went down that I want to protect you full time if you're going to continue the show."

"I know I threw out that idea about us working together, but when I saw you with that gun, I knew you were in your element. Continue to work with the Brotherhood. They need you more than I do."

"I'll let you two figure things out. I'll call you in the morning." Lincoln jogged away.

Reade ran a finger over her chin, causing heat waves down her spine. "I want to be wherever you are, and I want to be the one to keep you safe."

She placed a hand on his face. "I love your beard."

He barked out a laugh.

"I also love you, and if I have learned anything from a failed marriage it's that you should be doing what you want for a living. I want to fix up houses for people in need. Cameras and an audience aren't required to do that. I've made connections. I can figure out a way to help with less of a spotlight."

"Are you sure?"

"This whole television idea had been Stuart's to begin with. I went along. It seemed like fun at first, even if it didn't end that way. I'm glad I took the chance. The show brought you to me, but I don't have to be on camera to be happy. I can be the person behind the scenes."

"Do we have to decide our career paths right now?"

It was her turn to laugh. "The only thing I need to know is that you will always be there for me."

"Sweetheart, I will be right beside you, keeping you safe for as long as you will allow me. You make me want to stay put for the first time in a very long time. Wherever you are is where I'll be."

She placed a kiss on his soft, warm lips. "Then take me back to the cabin. Take me home."

ALSO BY STACEY WILK

No More Darkness

Through the Darkness

The Brotherhood Protectors World

Winter's Last Chance

The Last Betrayal

Her Last Word

The Last Days of Christmas

The Heritage River Series

A Second Chance House

The Bridge Home

The Essence of Whiskey and Tea

Special Forces: Operation Alpha World

Stage Fright

The Omega Team World

Silent Water

The Gabriel Hunter Series (middle grade)

Welcome to Kata-Tartaroo

Welcome to Bibliotheca

Welcome to Skull Mountain

ABOUT STAEY WILK

From an early age, Stacey Wilk told tales as a way to escape. At six she wrote short stories in composition notebooks, at twelve she wrote a novel on a typewriter, in high school biology she wrote rock star romances in her binder instead of paying attention.

But it wasn't until many years later, inspired by her children and a looming birthday, that she finally took her story-telling seriously. And published her first novel in 2013. Since then, she's gone on to publish fourteen more so women everywhere could fall in love and find an escape of their own.

She isn't done telling stories. Not by a long shot. If you want to read her emotional and honest books about family, romance, and second chances, visit her at www.staceywilk.com

To see what she writes next, follow her Facebook group for her amazing readers –
Stacey's Novel Family https://bit.ly/2FK8Lae
Or join her newsletter - https://bit.ly/2A0jEFk

BROTHERHOOD PROTECTORS

ORIGINAL SERIES BY ELLE JAMES

Brotherhood Protectors Series

Montana SEAL (#1)

Bride Protector SEAL (#2)

Montana D-Force (#3)

Cowboy D-Force (#4)

Montana Ranger (#5)

Montana Dog Soldier (#6)

Montana SEAL Daddy (#7)

Montana Ranger's Wedding Vow (#8)

Montana SEAL Undercover Daddy (#9)

Cape Cod SEAL Rescue (#10)

Montana SEAL Friendly Fire (#11)

Montana SEAL's Mail-Order Bride (#12)

SEAL Justice (#13)

Ranger Creed (#14)

Delta Force Rescue (#15)

Montana Rescue (Sleeper SEAL)

Hot SEAL Salty Dog (SEALs in Paradise)

Hot SEAL Hawaiian Nights (SEALs in Paradise)

ABOUT ELLE JAMES

ELLE JAMES also writing as MYLA JACKSON is a *New York Times* and *USA Today* Bestselling author of books including cowboys, intrigues and paranormal adventures that keep her readers on the edges of their seats. With over eighty works in a variety of sub-genres and lengths she has published with Harlequin, Samhain, Ellora's Cave, Kensington, Cleis Press, and Avon. When she's not at her computer, she's traveling, snow skiing, boating, or riding her ATV, dreaming up new stories. Learn more about Elle James at www.ellejames.com

Website | Facebook | Twitter | GoodReads | Newsletter | BookBub | Amazon

Follow Elle!
www.ellejames.com
ellejames@ellejames.com

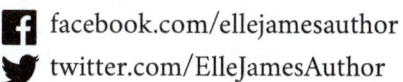

facebook.com/ellejamesauthor
twitter.com/ElleJamesAuthor

www.ingramcontent.com/pod-product-compliance
Lightning Source LLC
Chambersburg PA
CBHW071253130626
46556CB00003B/1295